JOSE EMILIO SALGADO

CALCIUM

THE FATE OF EARTH AND MANKIND TOLD BY AN
ATOM WHO SAW IT ALL HAPPEN

Author: Salgado, José Emilio
Calcium: the fate of Earth and mankind, told by an atom who saw it all happen. –
1a ed. Franco Azar & Cia. 2011.
Translated by: Peter Gold
ISBN-13: 978-9872719616 (Calcium)
ISBN-10: 9872719616
1. Narrative Argentina. I. Gold, Peter, trad. II. Título.
CDD A863

Original Title: Calcio Biografía de un átomo

Author: José Emilio Salgado

© 2011, José Emilio Salgado

© 2011, Franco Azar & Cia S.A. / www.upaediciones.com

Translated by: Peter Gold

Illustrated by: Maria Matilde Bossi

Contribution by: Karina Bonifatti

ISBN 978-987-27196-1-6

To my grand children

INTRODUCTION

The new Hayden Planetarium in New York is a cube with sides of steel and glass. An enormous sphere is supported in the centre of the building. Around it, covering the whole of the ground floor, an exhibition on the Cosmos and the Atomic World explains the mysteries of the infinitely large and reveals the secrets of the incredibly small. Hanging globes suspended in space represent the stars and planets, while in another section the atoms are shown with the nucleus at the centre and the electrons revolving around them in concentric orbits.

One of the visitors, thinking that I know something about the subject, asks me to help him find the representations of the Sun and the Earth from amongst the group of spheres. When I point them out to him, I suggest that he looks at them as they really are: two particles lost in the Cosmos. One, bright and yellow, the other, smaller, pale and blue.

The spectacle of the sky shows us thousands of millions of stars that make up the Milky Way, just one more galaxy among the almost infinite number that form the Universe. In a map of the heavens we can see the majestic spirals of the galaxies and the enormous distances between them. To the right of the Southern Cross the star closest to the Solar System can be seen: Alpha Centauri. What we see is a picture of it more than four years old – the time that it takes to reach the Earth at the speed of light.

I say to the visitor:

"The panorama of the sky is in fact a collection of old photographs, each one taken at a different time, like a great collage. The scene is shared by images which are not contemporary: we see the brightest star, Sirius, as it was more than eight years ago, and one of the most distant galaxies, made up of more than a hundred thousand million stars, shows us what it looked like two million years earlier. When this image began its journey through space, human beings did not yet exist on Earth. The vision of the sky is like a trick photo in which my grandson would appear standing next to me but I would be wearing short trousers and be the same age as him in a photo taken in my childhood."

Then we stop in the world of the infinitely small and something arouses my curiosity. This sector of the exhibition describes the size of the atoms, their structure and the process of their formation. Inspired by the images that we were both looking at, I explain to the visitor that the hydrogen atoms that form part of our body were born with the Universe more than ten thousand million years ago and that all of the other elements that we are made of – carbon, oxygen, sodium and the rest – were born thousands of millions of years ago in the centre of old stars that no longer exist.

I hadn't thought about it before. In certain instances my mind behaves in a strange way. An idea crosses my mind, it goes back and forth and I pay no attention to it, until one day the unexpected happens: the idea acquires an identity that I hadn't expected and completely changes my way of interpreting it.

I say goodbye to the visitor and start to climb the spiral walkway that winds around the sphere of the planetarium. I look at the hanging globes without seeing them, my mind wandering elsewhere.

I decide to return to my hotel. As I leave the sky tells me that it is about to snow. The twilight paints the clouds with changing colours in tones of orange and green. A taxi takes me to the Delmonico in Park Avenue. In my apartment on the eleventh floor the voice of Tony Bennett envelops me with the tune of *I left my heart in San Francisco* and through the magic of memory scenes of thirty years earlier appeared as if they were happening at that moment. With a drink in my hand and the first flakes of snow falling on the road, my thoughts return to the disquieting idea that I had that afternoon, in which atoms that are almost everlasting make up my whole being and are the same ones that give form to my glass and to the snow that is swirled by the wind against the window-pane.

I don't know why but at that moment I am thinking about only one of them: a calcium atom and where and when it was born and how it got as far as me.

That night in February 1999 this story was born.

PART ONE

FROM HEAVEN TO EARTH

If, in some cataclysm, all of scientific knowledge were to be destroyed, and only one sentence passed on to the next generation of creatures what statement would contain the most information in the fewest words? I believe it is the atomic hypothesis (or the atomic fact, or whatever you wish to call it) *that all things are made of atoms – little particles that move around in perpetual motion, attracting each other when they are a little distance apart, but repelling upon being squeezed into one another.*

Richard Feynman, *Six Easy Pieces*

****

The stars seem immutable but they are not. They are born, evolve and die like living organisms... If the star is massive enough...the ultimate collapse is a catastrophic event..... a great explosion which disperses to space most of the elements manufactured in its interior during its lifetime....The earth and we owe our corporeal existence to events which took place billions of years ago in stars that lived and died long ago before the solar system came into being

ROBERT JASTROW, *Stars, planets and life*

1

THE BIRTH

This story begins a little more than a thousand million years ago somewhere in the Universe. It happened in an instant: a point in the sky lit up with a light as bright as that of thousands of suns all shining at once. It was followed by an enormous explosion that destroyed a huge star.

I don't know if you know that hydrogen and helium atoms were born at the same time as the Universe, but that those of other known chemical species were formed and are still formed in the centre of giant stars in the last stage of their existence. In these enormous factories hydrogen atoms first become helium atoms and then these combine together to create other atoms: silicon, carbon, oxygen and so on.

A short time after that explosion the star had turned into great clouds of very bright dust and gas which spread throughout space in different directions at a speed of thousands of kilometers per second. As you can imagine, in one of these clouds and amongst the countless particles that were travelling in it, was our atom.

At first he found it hard to realize that he was an individual. But as time passed and with contact with other particles like himself he became aware of his atomic condition, so that a few days later he started to utter his first words. That was when a carbon atom came up to him and said:

"How do you feel? I'm still shocked by the terrible time that we went through in the star before the explosion."

The calcium atom seemed to stutter but didn't say anything.

The carbon atom persisted:

"Haven't you got a name yet? What should I call you? What about Cal ?"

Just then he heard other atoms around him chanting his name:

"Cal... Cal... Cal..."

He was so overcome that he thought his structure, with its nucleus and their electrons, was about to fall apart. But that didn't happen and right away they started to try out their atomic games together, bumping into each other and rushing around from one side to another. They were the first adventures of the new born.

The cloud of dust and gas in which they were travelling – that small part of the matter that was expelled by the star when it exploded – continued its journey through space with an unknown destination, as if looking for somewhere in the Universe where it could deposit such a precious load.

At this early stage Cal found it very helpful to listen to the hydrogen and helium atoms, who were all very old, and to one of them in particular, Hydrogen, a very wise atom who, as well as introducing them to the secrets of the creation of the Universe and the laws that determined their fate, explained to them that the explosion of the giant star had taken place on the edge of a galaxy, the Milky Way.

Hydrogen liked to say to them:

"My dear little ones, you and I are now star dust and we shall travel through space for a long time, perhaps for five hundred years. We are now a few light years away from the star group Alpha Centauri. By my calculation and given the path we are taking we are probably being attracted towards them. If this is not the case, the other possible destination is a single star: the Sun."

Old Hydrogen liked to frighten them and told them in great detail how they would disintegrate if they ended up being trapped at the end of their journey through space by one of the stars that was waiting for them....Then, seeing that they were terrified by that prospect and to give them some hope, he softened his story and told them that the cloud might possibly meet up with an wayward asteroid or a comet. If they passed near the asteroid they could be attracted by its force of gravity and in that case they would be stuck to its body like parasites for the rest of their existence, wandering around the Universe forever.

Thirty years after the explosion that occurred at the beginning of this story the cloud's journey through space was continuing as before. But the young atoms had changed a great deal. They had found different ways of having fun. The reason was because the atoms are attracted to other atoms, causing them to join up together. When they join the atoms share their electrons, which stay bonded together and form a new particle.

Cal was seized by the desire to join others and once he had decided that he was going to do so he started to look for his would-be companions. He went up to two chlorine atoms and exchanged meaningful glances with them (atomic glances, of course), but he didn't dare do anything. For a couple of years – seconds for him – he wandered aimlessly around the cloud, unable to choose between the myriads of atoms of other species until, when he least expected it, fate made him choose an oxygen atom. Or did the oxygen atom choose him?

So Cal and Oxygen formed a new particle: a molecule of calcium oxide. To be precise, I should say that from that union everything changed for them: they shared every moment and the years passed quickly. They looked at the sight of the sky around them, picturing a common destiny forever and scoffing at Hydrogen's terrifying prophecies.

When Cal reached his two-hundredth birthday his doubts about the destination of his journey had gone: they weren't going to fall into Alpha Centauri. Their path was taking them inexorably towards the Sun, a tiny insignificant star.

Everyone thought that it was a cruel twist of fate that having been born in the vastness of the Milky Way, full of beautiful and important places, they would end up in such an unknown, out-of-the-way suburb of the galaxy.

As is the case with things in space, it happened very suddenly: in the distance the lengthy image of an asteroid appeared, cylindrical in shape and about thirty kilometers long by eight kilometers wide. It was old and covered in small craters like acne scars on a young man's face. The cloud of dust continued on its path and the asteroid approached with the indifference that asteroids always show, as if they were going to go right through you without realizing you were there. Cal and Oxygen tried to work out where their paths would meet and pushed into other molecules with the aim of moving towards the asteroid. Their intention was clear: they were trying to be attracted to it by the gravitational pull of this tiny heavenly body in order to escape the hell that awaited them if they reached the Sun. It wasn't a bad idea at all.

However their effort was in vain. The pull of the asteroid was very weak and the few kilometers that separated them from it meant that they didn't even feel its effect. Millions of the cloud's molecules that were nearer clung on to its wrinkled surface and began a journey of thousands of years. And that's where they stayed, keeping very still in case a false move separated them from the cosmic traveller that had come to rescue them.

The size of the Sun appeared to grow as Cal and Oxygen got closer to it and about a hundred years after the encounter with the asteroid it had become a yellow disk that stood out from the other stars. Later other spheres appeared with different sizes and colours, reflecting the light of the Sun and revolving around it in elliptical orbits. One of them was surrounded by strange rings, but of all of them Cal was fascinated by a small, pale, blue one.

Hydrogen explained to them that what they were seeing was a planetary system that went round the Sun, and also told them that this type of collection of star and planets was very common in the Universe.

Our atoms were scared as the closeness of the Sun meant that the end was near. They couldn't face the thought that they would fall into it and be destroyed. They had to find a way out.

As they had done so often before they turned to the experience of Hydrogen.

"How can we escape the pull of the star?"

"I recommend the same thing to everyone: try to get close to the planets, you may get attracted by one of them. The Sun means your inevitable destruction, but the other bodies seem to be harmless."

The cloud of stellar dust began to turn towards the Sun and continued like that for tens of years. Later it divided itself into smaller clouds which, as a result of the gravity of the planets and the path of their orbits, started to settle on the Sun or on one of its planets: Jupiter, Saturn, Mars, and Earth.

Cal and Oxygen were living through a crucial moment in the great cosmic game of destiny.

Finally they were attracted by the blue sphere: Earth. As they approached they bumped thousands of times against other molecules, against nitrogen and oxygen. The bumps had the same effect as a parachute: they fell slowly through the layer of gases which was the Earth's atmosphere.

The slowness of the descent gave them the chance to study for the first time the dazzling sight before them: the small blue sphere had become an enormous ball with a surface that changed from grey to brown with large patches of green and blue.

When they got closer it seemed as though the surface began to wrinkle into mountains, in contrast to the smoothness of vast plains.

The journey through space was coming to an end. But before I tell you how it ended you need to know that by the time that Cal arrived the Earth had already finished being formed as a planet. Although there were still some strong tremors in its crust, the oceans and the continents were already distinguishable on its surface.

An atom of oxygen from the atmosphere who they bumped into on their way down and who sympathized with his fellow atom on seeing him so scared, gave them some advice:

"Try to fall into the water, it'll be best for you."

"What's water?" asked Oxygen anxiously.

"Everything you can see that's green."

They moved swiftly and successfully. They flew over the green ocean for a while and saw how its surface was rippled by the wind until finally they hit the wall of a wave and went into the water.

Then something unexpected happened: the hydrogen and oxygen atoms that formed the water molecules attacked them furiously. They tried to defend themselves but it was useless. The ocean seemed to be boiling at this point and the heat was unbearable.

It is no better for atoms than for humans: so many years spent travelling together through space, sharing the highs and the lows, and it takes just a second for something to separate them for good. Cal felt naked. Not only had he lost Oxygen in the fight but he had also lost two of his twenty electrons, which meant that he was electrically unbalanced. With more positive than negative charges in his body something even more significant had happened, something that affected his identity. Cal had ceased to be a calcium atom and had turned into a calcium ion. It was no better for Oxygen: he was trapped between a group of hydrogen and oxygen atoms and they made him join himself to them by exchanging his electrons. He was turned into an hydroxyl ion, a poor hydroxyl ion.

After a few minutes Cal started to move freely. In his new state he felt more important and even stronger. He was surrounded by hundreds of molecules of water and this gave him the sensation that in fact they were protecting him. And once he had got over this initial moment, something that is always confusing and raises all kinds of doubts, he could start fully to enjoy his freedom.

Cal was very young. He had only just turned five hundred and three.

2

LIFE IN THE OCEAN

When Cal arrived on the Earth there was no life on the planet, apart from the first bacteria. His only companions in the ocean were the water molecules and the ions of dissolved salts. After he had got to know them well he mainly liked the chlorides and sulphates and in particular he competed with the sodiums and the potassiums. He enjoyed himself most near the surface, in the transparent and restless waters where he felt comforted by the diffuse and mysterious light of the Sun, because when Cal went down to the depths of the sea he felt frightened; the light disappeared and he had to struggle to see the seabed, where he discovered valleys and mountains, great plains and smooth slopes covered in sand, dark chasms where the light would never reach. Sometimes he was shaken by a volcanic eruption; the waters became agitated and cloudy and for two or three years he had to feel his way around. Fortunately everything then went back to how it was before; the water became clear and the light of the Sun came through once again to give him warmth and confidence.

Whenever he could he rose to the surface, let himself be rocked by the waves and stared at the sky. Then Cal remembered his first image of the Earth, that pale blue dot that was scarcely visible against the blackness of the heavens. Sometimes some of the water molecules around him took the opportunity to fly; they speeded up their movements and detached themselves from their companions and mingled with the air. Cal tried to copy them, but he couldn't. So he had to resign himself to watching them drift away on the wind. That's when the hydrogen and oxygen atoms of the water molecules said goodbye to him, often laughing and joking. That shouldn't surprise us, since they were the privileged inhabitants of the ocean: from the air they had the power to observe the surface of dry land, the vast plains divided by small brooks or wide rivers, long mountain chains, some with snowy peaks. What they saw were pictures of a deserted planet, still without signs of vegetation or animal life and crossed only by dust storms that blotted out the Sun. That's why the spectacle not only moved them but also terrified them, and the ocean turned into the home to which they all wanted to return as quickly as possible.

In certain circumstances the water molecules that were in the air started to group together and shortly afterwards they hurriedly formed a cloud and continued their journey together. The clouds had different shapes: there were cumulus, cirrus, or some stretched out like very long strata with a shapeless outline. They were white or grey and seemed to float in the sky. When the Sun disappeared behind the distant horizon, they became stained with other colours; they were no longer white and grey but orange, with violet highlights, and they wore multi-coloured clothes.

The sudden changes of temperature caused another phenomenon: the tiny drops of water from the cloud formed larger heavier drops that could no longer float in the air and fell as rain. Realizing that they could not control where they would fall, the atoms became concerned about being part of a rain drop. If they fell in the sea or in some river, they would feel safe; but if the hit the dry ground they were very worried because most likely they would go far down into the earth until they reached an aquifer or an underground river, where many of them would remain trapped for centuries.

When they returned from their travels the hydrogen and oxygen atoms used to dazzle Cal with their tales. In one of these stories, which to him sounded as if they were made up, they told him with great conviction that the water molecules not only had the gift of turning into vapour and being able to fly but also had the ability to join together in solid, compact masses. In fact they turned into snow or ice and sailed along in an ice-floe or slept in a glacier. Cal found it hard to believe them but later he would discover that they were telling the truth.

One of his happiest moments at that time was when, having been swept along by the wind and the sea currents, he reached the coast. He did not know what solid ground was like, but at last he could see it from close to. For the first time he thought he would be able to touch it. The waves carried him along for weeks on end. High cliffs plunged down on to the rocky, sandless shore. Cal wanted to see everything all at once; he was keen to fill his thoughts with different shapes. Then the inevitable happened. After much toing and froing, the ocean abandoned him and he couldn't get back; he was left swimming in a small pool, right on the flat surface of a huge rock that lay by the edge of the water. The next wave couldn't reach him and neither could the next one. With each wave that broke against the rocks the sea seemed to get further away.

The Sun was now high and he felt its strong rays, making the temperature almost unbearable, something that Cal had not felt since the day he fell into the sea with Oxygen. A little while later, because of the heat, the water molecules started to leave him, mixing with the air before disappearing. For their part the dissolved ions approached one another and bumped into each other. In this ever decreasing pool Cal clung to two chlorides who gave him a puzzled look, and when all the water molecules had gone, they remained clinging to the rock as if they were stuck to it, unable to move. Yes, they had turned into a small patch of salt on the dark stone.

It is fair to say that for the first time in his life Cal felt something that he had never felt before: calm. His natural state had always been constant movement. Either alone or with Oxygen, our atom had glided between the particles of cosmic dust, had jumped up and down as he bumped into the atmosphere and dived in the depths of the ocean, but he had never stopped, not for an instant! It's not hard to understand, therefore, why the peace that he felt was a very strange sensation for him and one which is almost impossible to describe.

However, after a few hours Cal adapted to this infinite calm and could spend time looking at the static cliffs and the projection of their shadows on the rocks on the beach. That is how he stayed during the whole of that day and part of the following one. In the clear, cloudless night he could look at the sky without anything getting in his way. His thoughts turned to the days just after his birth, to the flight through space, to the asteroid that almost captured him, to the years spent with Oxygen...

At dawn the sea beat strongly against the shore once more. After a few attempts he was rescued by a very high wave with a crest of foam on top. He said goodbye to the two chlorides, said a few appropriate words to the atoms of the rock and, surrounded by a lot of water molecules, he danced with them as he celebrated his return home. Cal had recovered his lost mobility.

At this point I should explain to the reader that the atoms that had joined together to form the Earth – long before Cal was born – defined two units to measure time, but without abandoning their atomic concept of universal time. These units arose out of their observations on the behaviour of the planet. The concept of "day", which they defined as the time that it takes for one full revolution of the Earth on its axis, came from the succession of dawns and sunsets, while the idea of "year", which was a unit equal to the time that it takes for the Earth to complete its orbit round the Sun, was inspired by the sequence of summers and winters. However, it didn't take long for them to realize that these units varied in relation to the constant of their atomic clocks and that this was due to the gravitational interaction between the earth and the Moon. So that when Cal and Oxygen fell into the ocean, a day lasted 18 hours and a year was 481 days. A thousand million years later – in our era – a day has 24 hours and a year has 365 days. Their observations, therefore, were quite correct: the pull of the Moon slows down the speed that the Earth rotates by two milliseconds per century.

But to continue with our story: for many thousands of years afterwards Cal experienced few frights but nor could he return to the shore to experience the sense of calm again. Until one day everything started to change. The process that I am about to describe took hundreds of millions of years and started one fine morning.

The rays of the sun, which filtered down just a few meters below the surface of the water where Cal was, suddenly disappeared. Something had cloaked him in shadow. He looked up and saw a very strange figure, made of more than twenty carbon, hydrogen, oxygen and nitrogen atoms. Yes, there was no doubt that it was a molecule, but of an unfamiliar size. Cal approached it slowly. He noted that it lumbered about and I must say that he was justified in feeling that its atoms were looking at him with contempt. This was the least they could do: they were part of something new, something out of the ordinary.

Impressed but trying to be nice, Cal managed with a great effort to get one of the carbon atoms to explain who they were, or rather what they were doing joined together in such a strange way. The carbon atom answered him directly:

"We are a different type of molecule from those that you are familiar with, we are nothing more nor less than… an amino acid!"

Cal was intrigued and asked him how long they had been organized like that and the carbon atom replied that the molecule had been formed a long time ago through a very complicated process that he couldn't or didn't care to explain. He added that he was surprised that Cal hadn't noticed it before. But that wasn't all. To differentiate itself from the water ions the carbon atom added:

"It's not what you think. We're not an inorganic particle – how could you think such a thing? We amino acids are something totally modern in the creation of the universe: we're organic molecules!"

For Cal – inorganic as he was and an example of order and balance – the definition was a real insult!

Initially very few of these molecules appeared but after a few years there were millions of them. And a thousand or ten thousand years later not only were there many more amino acids, but proteins appeared in the sea. These molecules were *really* big. They were formed by several amino acids linking together to form chains and rolls of unusual shapes.

From then on Cal witnessed an explosion of life in the ocean: the proteins had joined up with other combinations of atoms to create small crustaceans, sponges, anemones which looked like flowers and with a range of different colours... Of course everything changed completely for Cal and became much more fun! He never ceased to be amazed by new creatures, especially their unusual size. With two of his chloride ion friends, the ones he had shared that adventure with on the rock by the shore, he often clung on to one of the smallest crustaceans and they let themselves be taken for a walk. They were very amused by the way that it fed itself.

Everything seemed to be going along very well until one fine day they noticed that a lot of water molecules and hundreds of ions had disappeared inside the crustacean. Cal and his chloride friends could not imagine what could have happened to them and they felt very concerned. They were particularly anxious about the fate of one of their playmates who had disappeared: a magnesium ion that they never saw again. From then on they agreed to observe the new inhabitants from a distance. If one of them approached, they let themselves be carried away by a thermal current that took them up to the surface of the sea and away from danger.

Long after this first experience in the sea the first fishes appeared: brown, blue, red or green, with gentle eyes and mouths that constantly opened and closed. At the bottom of the sea there were also dozens of other different creatures moving about: sea snails, lobsters, crabs, oysters, squid, octopus and the incredible sea horses.

Ions like Cal and the oxygen and hydrogen atoms of the water molecules found it difficult to understand what was happening. Were these other oxygens and hydrogens – the ones that appeared in that way – really the same as them? They seemed to recognize a great number of carbon atoms, although when they saw them combined into increasingly complex molecules and amazing combinations they were not sure that that is what they were. They were not sure that they were the atoms that they had known.

But they came to accept them. The evolution of Nature had created these living creatures with their different shapes and colours using very few parts – not more than thirty different types of atoms to which they themselves belonged. The carbons that formed this fish and that sea snail were indeed the same carbons.

3

THE GREAT DISCOVERY

The development of animal life, which until then had only occurred in the sea, began to extend to the land surface of the Earth. It started about three hundred and fifty million years ago. Later some fish appeared that Cal had never seen before, which had a particular characteristic: they had lungs that enabled them to breathe out of the water and strong fins that they used like paws. They were the first amphibians. As if this was not enough of a surprise, every so often natural evolution produced a new species which was different and more complex.

Cal and his friends followed this process as occasional spectators and although they couldn't see much from the water, from the information they received they got the impression that events similar to those that had occurred over thousands of centuries in the sea were taking place on dry land. That was the amazing thing: trillions of atoms just like them were taking part in this brand-new adventure of creation. In truth new tales were being woven century by century, but one – perhaps the most interesting one - was that countless water molecules, with their hydrogen and oxygen atoms, had fallen as rain on a very green area of the planet and now made up part of plants and trees. They climbed up by their roots, slid up the trunk and then through the leaves evaporated once more and returned to the atmosphere. Some, however, were trapped. Such adventures were related with great enthusiasm by the atoms of these molecules every time they returned from dry land. They were the hosts of all of the atom get-togethers that were organized in the sea and Cal and his friends were nearly always there. In those days their stories about the former desert planet now being a garden caused a sensation. This was not surprising: they were describing a world that was very different from the one that all the atoms were used to.

One of the heroines of these stories was chlorophyll, a very large molecule with more than one hundred and thirty atoms of carbon, hydrogen, oxygen, nitrogen and magnesium, which when activated by sunlight produced reactions which, it must be admitted, Cal found hard to understand. Because of the chlorophyll many water molecules were broken up into atoms: the hydrogen ones on one side and the oxygen ones on the other, rather like the separation of Cal and Oxygen when they fell into the sea. Due to the action of the light the hydrogen atoms were combined with carbon dioxide taken from the air to make other substances in a long chain of chemical reactions that almost always ended in cellulose, the material that forms the structure of plants. A few steps more and the old hydrogen atoms would stop forming a molecule of water and turn into part of the branch of a tree and remain bound to it for many years. By contrast their old friends, the oxygen atoms, were freed and escaped back into the atmosphere to fly non-stop just like they did in their youth.

Since the arrival of Cal on Earth, there was constant movement of the tectonic plates that make up the surface of the planet (its crust) and that float on a fluid and viscous mantle. It was a slow, indiscernible movement, except for the almost perpetual observers like the atoms. When the different plates met and pushed against each other they formed mountain ranges or deep hollows that were filled with water. It will take about three hundred million years for the masses of all the continents to slowly merge into just one, called Pangaea, which covered one quarter of the planet and was surrounded by a single, enormous ocean. The flying atoms were the ones who reported these movements, and like geographers brought the new positions up to date every thousand years. It was actually a subject that kept them entertained for ages. They were joined by a group of cartographers who described the position of the continents with virtual maps. It also amused them to make predictions on how the process would end up: the majority correctly decided that all the lands would join up into a single one. Pangaea remained stable for some time but then the movements of the tectonic plates started once more, their surface split up and at the end of a long process the continental masses and the oceans ended up in the position that we know today.

At a time that we would consider to be contemporary if we were atoms and if we measured years lived in millions – one or two million years ago – something important happened one summer's day that would have major consequences for Cal. That afternoon the first reports reached the sea of the appearance of a new species of the animals that lived on the Earth. The small handful of the recently discovered species stood out from the others because its members went about on two legs and appeared to possess certain hitherto unknown faculties. Those who lived in the sea didn't pay much attention to this news and it could even be said that for thousands of years they completely ignored it. Their real interest only started not more than fifty thousand years ago when the new species already covered all of the continents and used natural caves to protect themselves from the other animals and from bad weather.

Word had it that they seemed very clever and intelligent. They made fire when they needed it and they could carve hard stones and turn them into knives, hammers or scrapers. As they did not yet know vessels or pots they camped near water in order to be able to drink easily by putting their face in it. They were nomadic and followed the path of their food – that of the animals that they would hunt in order to eat.

In Cal's conversations with his friends they couldn't help making comparisons between the new species and the dinosaurs which had dominated life on the planet for one hundred and sixty million years before they became extinct. Their favourite topic of discussion – including betting on it – was whether the new species would manage to last as long as or even longer than the dinosaurs. Cal bet that they wouldn't. But a barium ion, an odd-ball in the sea and an inveterate gambler who bet on everything, said:

"I bet you that these animals, who are much more intelligent, will find a way of surviving for much longer."

"What shall we bet?" asked Cal.
Barium answered right back:

"The one who loses has to stay at the bottom of the sea for a thousand years without seeing the light of the Sun."

"Doesn't that seem a lot to you?"

"I like to bet big," replied Barium.

"Okay. But there's just one problem."

"What's that?"

"We'll have to wait a hundred and sixty million years to find out who won!"

A short time later Cal was about to win the bet: the planet started to freeze. For various reasons the air temperature dropped over several centuries until it got very low and started an ice age that would last for ten thousand years. Cal recalled other similar experiences that had occurred in the sea but he had not attached much importance to them. According to the atoms in the atmosphere it was an impressive sight: the masses of polar ice moved in the form of glaciers more than a kilometer high and slowly covered the continents. The level of the oceans dropped by about a hundred meters and part of them froze over. A good number of residents of the sea could not tolerate it and so the population fell considerably. Some species disappeared for good. It was no better for the plants and the living creatures on the land; the cave-dwellers migrated to the equatorial regions where the conditions were more tolerable and many of them stopped off on the way.

In spite of such a disaster the human beings were able to survive and when, twelve thousand years later, this ice age came to an end, human evolution continued uninterrupted. Centuries later in Mesopotamia and in Egypt the first cities appeared and the atoms were shocked by the attributes that the new species began to show. Although Cal and his friends tried to draw conclusions from their behaviour, they hadn't yet managed to understand what it meant. That was when Cal's interest in humans began to grow. Until that moment the human race had been a hobby, but now he felt a great sense of curiosity about them, almost like what a child might feel when he discovers that there are other continents and he wants to fly to see them.

And so, fascinated by the stories that he was hearing, he asked himself the question that would determine the next few centuries of his life. Why not be part of a human body? Why not at least try? He knew that it would be very difficult but nothing persuaded him that it was impossible. After all, are human beings not made up of atoms?

He was so excited by the idea that he decided to discuss it with an old hydrogen atom that formed part of one of the molecules that accompanied him. His wisdom reminded him of his teacher of the early years. The old atom gave him an unequivocal reply:

"Cal, you do not realize how fortunate you have been to remain in the sea for so long and to be free. The vast majority of calcium atoms on the planet are slaves, they are chained, immobile, and they will be like that for ever. Some of those cliffs that you liked so much to look at are made up of limestone or dolomites, in other words of atoms just like you. The same is true of deposits of gypsum and other minerals, including the mortar in the buildings built by humans. An important part of all of them is made up of atoms like you, who didn't have the good fortune to fall into the sea."

Cal protested:

"But it's not the same in human beings..."

"Something similar happened with them. To be honest, I have to tell you that the only reference I have is the story of the atoms in a molecule of water that were part of a human body. They told me some amazing stories, but they didn't stay there for very long. They entered in a drink of water and left two days later with the urine, so you have to treat their opinion with care – as you can imagine there was a lot that they wouldn't have got to see. But I remember one important thing: they told me that the majority of the calcium atoms are trapped in bones, which are rigid structures that hold the bodies together. In other words, if you manage to become part of a human being, which for a start I don't think will be at all easy, you'll remain immobilized in any event. It's true that you would be able to move around everywhere as part of the body, and that would probably be fun, but you will still lose your freedom. In addition there's something that we haven't mentioned and which is fundamental, or the most serious point of all: human beings are like fleeting stars, they do not live for very long at all, less than one hundred years. That's nothing! Your stay in one of them will be a very brief moment in your existence – mere seconds. And to satisfy your curiosity, which I find rather childish, you're going to run the undue risk of ending up buried like the calcium atoms of dolomites."

Hydrogen's arguments were demoralizing, but Cal was determined to try it.

"Hydrogen, don't be offended. I respect your experience and that's why I asked you, but you have just said that your knowledge of humans is limited and that the most direct thing that you know about them comes from the story of some atoms from some molecule of water or another who were part of a body for just a few hours. Are you sure that calcium atoms cannot escape from bones? Forgive my insistence, but the truth is that even with everything that you've told me I would like to try."

"As you wish," Hydrogen replied. "But before you take your decision I want to finish giving you my advice, and maybe you'll end up changing your mind. The fact is that humans usually bury their dead. When the body that you're in dies, you're going to end up with it under the earth. If you are in any other part of the body and not in one of the bones you might manage to get free straight away and return to the cycle of Nature. You'll become part of something else and maybe even return to the sea. But if you're part of a bone, which is the most likely, you'll stay there for heaven knows how long... So my advice, dear friend, is to carry on as you are and don't rush into things. You are still young and you have a long existence ahead of you. All in all, it may be that everything I have said sounds exaggerated, because the likelihood of you forming part of a human being is very small."

Hydrogen's last words made some impression on Cal. Although he appreciated his advice and felt grateful, he was also aware that on the other hand he was getting a bit fed up with life in the sea. The movements of the earth's crust had ceased to interest him for some time. The volcanic eruptions had almost completely disappeared. He knew all the fish imaginable by heart... he was tired of their bulging eyes and their mouths that didn't stop moving. In fact he realized that he was also bored with all the other creatures that lived in the sea…. What else could you expect! He didn't like to say this to Hydrogen in order not to bother him, but what would happen if a fish suddenly swallowed him up or - even worse - one of those tiny ridiculous crustaceans that had made Magnesium disappear? Besides, Cal was about to turn a thousand million years old; he was just reaching maturity. It didn't seem reasonable to resign himself to routine. And for how long?

4

AN INEXCUSABLE LAPSE

Throughout the last millennium the ocean currents had taken Cal to the Cantabrian Sea, off the coast of Asturias in the north of Spain.

One summer morning in 1931, Cal was enjoying the sunlight that created reflections and shadows as it entered the water. It seemed to be a day like any other. However, that day would put an end to his routine of thousands of years.

Since he had decided over fifty centuries earlier to become part of a human being, his attempts had been unsuccessful. A few days before he had tried it once more: a ship passed close by and Cal had tried to stick to the hull but the turbulent sea had prevented him from doing so. Once more he thought about his fate and, with a sense of resignation, decided to wait.

He was thinking about this when the unexpected happened. The bright eyes of a small sea bream appeared in front of him. As his mouth approached, Cal remained stock still, as if hypnotized by the fish's gaze. It happened in a flash: the sunlight disappeared and the tiny mouth, which opened to swallow some water, gobbled him up. He couldn't believe what had happened, but there was nothing he could have done to prevent it.

He recalled his experiences with the first crustaceans, then with the fish, the games he used to play with the chloride atoms, Magnesium's disappearance.... And now? A whole life's experience wasted in an inexcusable moment of carelessness!

The atoms of the water molecules next to Cal tried to encourage him.

"Don't worry, we'll get out into the sea again, it's only for a second."

But something told him that it wasn't going to be like that, that he wasn't going to be able to escape. An unknown force gave him a push. As he went through a wall in the form of a membrane, its atoms looked at him pityingly. As he passed, one of them said to him:

"This fish is very small; he's growing a lot and he takes in all the atoms he can so that his body will grow. The ones that go through this intestinal wall are trapped; there's no way out."

And that's how it was. He clung on to other atoms, which in this case were phosphorus and oxygen, and after a few minutes (or was it hours?) they entered a tiny bone. They had just formed a molecule of calcium phosphate and they were stuck there alongside thousands of others.

From then on Cal was part of the small sea bream. He shook with his every movement and felt like his slave. Having been used to reckoning time in centuries, he started to count it in minutes. He had dreamt for more than five thousand years of becoming part of a human being and getting to know the secrets of his body, but he had ended up in the bone of a young fish, which condemned him to remain in the sea. Was there ever a more miserable atom?

The fact is that in the end he was lucky: the bone was very small and this enabled him to move about. The fish moved so quickly that with each swish of its tail it made the little bone sway within its body. On the other hand Cal received basic, confusing signals from the sea bream's little brain, which as you know only controls its instincts – to defend and attack, to get food, to reproduce and to perpetuate the species. But as time passed he came to accept them. This was also due to something else, which gave him some comfort: he thought about what Hydrogen had said about human beings, that they were short-lived creatures, whose lives lasted for a brief moment... And so Cal tried to cheer himself up with the thought of how short the life of a fish must be compared to that of a human. Besides, having seen so many of them in the sea he knew that fish did not bury their dead, so he came to the great conclusion that he would just need a bit of patience and he would soon be free again.

In this brief period, which was rather like a spell in prison, Cal learned a lot. Up until then he had been free; he had felt things directly, without intermediaries. Now the whole of his relationship with the external world took place solely through the senses of the little fish. His eyes saw via him, his body transmitted the temperature of the water, his sudden movements shook both him and the bone... This experience, which was quite difficult at first, would prove very useful later on, as we shall see.

Phosphorus, a neighbouring atom in the calcium phosphate molecule, was the one who helped him most to adapt. Phosphorus was very introverted; he could spend weeks on end without uttering a word. In this respect at least his personality was the opposite of Cal's. However, the difference between the two atoms didn't prevent them from striking up a friendship which, fortunately, would not be a brief one.

Phosphorus was much older than Cal; he was about five thousand million years old and had arrived in the Solar System when it was beginning to be formed. On the few occasions that he spoke he talked about the fact that initially the Sun didn't shine. "It was a compact mass of hydrogen that in time would become a star," he used to say, before falling back into silence, which is in any case so typical of phosphorous atoms.

One day, however, after his relationship with Cal had become closer, Phosphorus told him more:

"An enormous disk, a mixture of star dust and gases that had come from distant parts of the Milky Way, revolved around the Sun. They took up a large area in space. I was in one of the microscopic particles of dust, joined to other atoms during the journey through the Cosmos. For millions of years the pull of gravity compressed the cloud of hydrogen and subjected its atoms to extremely high pressures and temperatures, until it reached the point when, in the centre of the sphere where the conditions were most critical, a nuclear reaction started. It was just like a hydrogen bomb but of stellar dimensions. The amount of energy released by the fusion of the atoms was enormous; its light lit up space and then the Sun started to shine. A few centuries later it was a normal, average-sized star, just like thousands of millions of stars that make up the galaxy."

Cal couldn't believe that his normally silent friend had been witness to such an event that happened four thousand five hundred million years earlier. The nuclear reaction, which is self-controlled, continues to this day giving out light and heat and will continue for a lot longer, perhaps for another five thousand million years. The whirling mass of dust and gases, which was diffuse at first, began to group together in different sized lumps, with the smallest nearest the Sun and the larger ones in more distant orbits.

According to what Phosphorus told him later, he and his dust particles were attracted by one of those lumps. They then felt the pressure of gravity pulling them together in a ball of fire. They were amongst the last to arrive and they landed on the burning surface. The Earth and the other planets had begun their long formative process. The temperature was so high that the particle, melted by the heat, turned into a viscous, almost liquid mass that was left floating adrift and shaken by constant tremors. They had to wait more than one thousand five hundred million years for the crust of the planet to cool down and for the continental plates to consolidate. Much later a significant part of the Earth's surface was covered by water and a new life began for Phosphorus and his friends at that time: they had found their home in the ocean.

The microscopic particle was insoluble and settled on the bottom. Centuries later, when the sea was teeming with life, one of the first microorganisms that prowled around took him in and so Phosphorus entered into a living creature for the first time. The microorganism soon served as food for another bigger one and so, along a chain that seemed endless to Phosphorus, he arrived in the little sea bream on the same day that Cal lost his liberty.

By the summer of 1933 Cal and Phosphorus had been bound to the bone for two years, and given the position that they were in they had little hope of getting free. Others had managed it but not them. However, one afternoon that year something happened that would change their lives forever.

The little fish, which Cal and Phosphorus called Bream, had grown into an adult and that morning he was swimming confidently next to one of his brothers. Both were agile, attractive, fine swimmers and stood out because of their strength and their daring. Suddenly the brother, who was swimming ahead, was dragged towards the surface by a strange force and in less than a minute he disappeared. When he saw what was happening, Bream shuddered, and although his body trembled with anxiety, he didn't stop swimming for one second. His instinct took over but at the same time confused him; on the one hand he felt afraid and wanted to get away, but on the other hand he was terribly hungry, for food was scarce and he had to compete for it with the other fish. At that precise moment of hunger he saw a clam moving nearby and threw himself furiously at it. As I said, no-one was faster or more daring than he was. While he was still enjoying its special flavour, he felt a terrible pain, as if someone had drilled a hole in his head. From then on everything was total confusion. He was pulled upwards by a force much greater than his own. Then he felt himself fly through the air and end up with a tremendous thud on a hard, hostile surface. He tried to breathe, but he couldn't. A few moments later he was dead.

Inside Bream everything was quiet. What had happened? Where were they? Cal wanted to talk to Phosphorus, but he saw that he was lost in thought and he didn't want to bother him. The fish's eyes could no longer see, which meant that Cal couldn't see through them either. The only thing he felt was a rhythmic movement, like the one that rocked him a long time ago on the surface of the sea when he played with the waves. He didn't know that the fish was dead, abandoned on the deck of a fishing boat.

There were five men in the boat's crew and the one who had caught Bream was the youngest. He was fifteen and was very strong, with square shoulders, a round face and very curly hair that the north wind tried to untangle. With an expert tug he pulled out the hook and threw Bream on top of the other fish that were piled up in the stern.

The skipper of the boat, Ricardo Vega, was from Asturias and just over forty years old but with a face that was furrowed in wrinkles from the Sun and the salty wind. The other crew members were Juan (his eldest son), Francisco (Paquito to his friends, the one with the round face and curly hair) and two other assistants who were also very young.

Ricardo looked at the stern and thought that the amount of fish was more than enough for a day's work. He pulled on the rudder and headed for the port. Half an hour later they tied up at a jetty in a little town on the Asturian coast.

Once the moorings were secured everyone set about loading the fish into baskets to be taken to the market. Juan separated the two sea bream, which were the best of the catch, slit them open to clean them and placed them in a basket.

Cal was worried; he had felt strange blows, then silence. The movement that reminded him of the waves in the sea had stopped.

Phosphorus was still distracted, while the other atoms of the molecule remained impassive; they were happy just to feel that they were still part of the small bone of a fish.

Now the movement returned: one, two, one, two, from side to side. This was a new rhythm for Cal. He was experiencing a human being walking for the first time. It was

Juan's steps along the jetty that were making the basket sway, with its load of the two best sea bream of the day.

PART TWO

AMONGST HUMANS

Man: term applied to our species, that is, rational mammals.
MARÍA MOLINER, *Diccionario de uso del Español*

To be immortal is unremarkable. Except for Man, all creatures are immortal because they know nothing of death; what is divine, terrible, incomprehensible, is to know oneself to be immortal. I have observed that, in spite of religion, this conviction is very rare. Jews, Christians and Muslims profess immortality, but the veneration in which they hold the first hundred years proves that that is all they believe in, since all the rest are forever destined to rewarding or punishing those years.
JORGE LUIS BORGES, *El inmortal*

A god is born. Others die. The Truth
Neither came nor went: what changed was Error.
Now we have another Eternity,
And what has passed was always better.
Blind, Knowledge works on hopeless ground.
Crazy, Faith lives the dream of its cult.

A new god is only a word.

Neither seek nor believe: everything is occult.

FERNANDO PESSOA, *Natal*

5

A NEW HOME

The Cantabrian wind blew down the narrow streets of the humble fishermen's quarter. The figure of Carmen, Ricardo Vega's wife, could be seen in the window of one of its houses. She was awaiting the return of her husband and sons; she knew that the weather had been calm and they had had a favourable wind.

She saw them walking along the jetty; the gusting wind caught Francisco's curly hair and carried his loud laughter to the hill of Barrio Alto.

As he went in Juan gave Carmen the basket with the two sea bream.

"Mother, they've already been cleaned. They're nice ones; put them on the grill."

"Juan, I've made some bean stew with clams for tonight."

"We'll burst, what with this heat and your beans. Please, leave the stew for tomorrow and cook the fish."

Carmen thought Juan was right: the heat was really unbearable. She'd have enough time while her husband and the boys had a bath and got changed. She fetched some wood to make up the fire and when it was ready she put the fish on the grill.

Cal and Phosphorus, who were in the smaller fish between the protein molecules of its flesh, stayed still, chained to other molecules just like theirs, that is, the thousands of calcium phosphates than made up the little bone. They didn't know what was happening. First they felt a few blows, then the temperature rose, making the protein molecules shake and releasing a lot of water molecules which quickly escaped as they were evaporated by the heat.

Meanwhile Carmen carefully laid the table; she set the plates and the cutlery, and placed a jug of wine, another of water and some rolls that she had cooked beneath the ashes in the hearth. When the bream were ready, she cut them into portions to fit them into a white dish with some boiled potatoes which she had just cooked.

Cal and Phosphorus were then shaken by a series of blows before things finally went quiet again. Suddenly shaken out of his lethargy, Phosphorus shot a worried look at Calcium and said:

"The only way we can find out what's going on is to arrange to communicate with the atoms on Bream's skin. They're in contact with the outside and can tell us where we are."

But Phosphorus's plan didn't work. There was tremendous confusion amongst the atoms and no-one took any notice of him. Not even the most inventive amongst them could have imagined that the fish that contained the bone had been turned into nothing more nor less than a tasty meal, and the future of all of them was dependent on the desires of the four people about to eat.

On the rustic table made of strips of plain wood, the porcelain dish displayed its contents of the two bream, boned and cut into mouth-sized pieces. Without waiting, Francisco spiked one of the pieces and swallowed it straight down. Inside it was Cal. Without realizing it he had entered the body of a human being.

"Paquito, be careful of the bones," warned his mother.

The piece of fish slipped down his throat until it reached the stomach, where Francisco's body started the digestive process. The proteins, fats and also the small fish bone were furiously attacked by enzymes and hydrochloric acid. They had to be transformed into more simple and soluble substances in order to be absorbed.

In seconds the bone was stripped of its proteins and was left exposed. After two years of confinement, Cal could at last see beyond the walls that surrounded him. And the first thing that he noticed was the thousands of chloride and hydrogen ions from the hydrochloric acid that were milling around him. He asked one of them, as if he knew him:

"Please, Chloride, could you tell me where I am? What's happening?"

His attacker's smile made him fear the worst.

"You're in Paquito Vega's stomach and there's no way you can escape."

The expression on Cal's face disconcerted the group, for it was one of joy and not fear.

"You mean I'm in a human's stomach? That's incredible!... Phosphorus, we've got into the body of a human being!"

Phosphorus, in whom Cal had confided his innermost desires, was pleased for his friend but was also worried about the fury of the attackers.

"Be careful, Cal, they want to split us up. Let's try to stick together."

Francisco's stomach worked tirelessly to complete the digestive process and in the midst of the task the bone could not resist the attack of the stomach's acids and enzymes. In truth it was an unequal fight that left Cal once more turned into an ion and surrounded by water molecules, a stranger lost in hostile surroundings. He couldn't find Phosphorus and he had no option but to let himself be carried along. After passing through some enormous flood gates that opened and closed without apparent reason, he had entered into an incredibly large tube. Its wrinkled walls were covered in a thick down. Yes, they had reached Francisco's intestine, which is why they were attacked by a different set of enzymes. But obviously the objective of the attackers was the same: to complete the digestion of the food with the aim of absorbing it.

Cal was one of the first: the hairs on the wall of the intestine trapped him straight away. First a gentle push, then a membrane that let him pass, and finally, the turbulent current of an unknown red liquid. He was swimming in the current without knowing where he was and without having the faintest idea where he was going. He was surrounded by a lot of his old friends, the water molecules, but also some new haughty, unflappable ones. In the midst of the torrent he thought he saw Phosphorus appear like a ghost, but then the image disappeared. Fortunately they eventually found each other again. There was no time for niceties:

"Where are we going to end up?" asked Phosphorus, who was nothing if not a logical atom.

"Maybe the current will deposit us somewhere in the body, otherwise we'll carry on like this, just going round everywhere," said Cal. "At least it looks as though the same thing is going to happen as when Bream swallowed us: we'll be staying put."

The answer became clear a few minutes later, when they entered a narrower artery which divided into even narrower ones. Phosphorus and Cal took the one that opened on the right. Once they were in it they went along it very slowly until they came out through a thin wall before entering another, almost colourless liquid that in a few seconds took them to the entrance to an enormous building where millions of calcium phosphate molecules awaited them. Maybe without thinking about it, maybe because they thought that history wouldn't repeat itself, Cal and Phosphorus went over to them. Not surprisingly they immediately stopped moving: the body had ceased to absorb them. They didn't even suspect it, but from that moment they would form part of a bone: Francisco's right shoulder blade.

To be honest, and as I already expected, the experience they had acquired inside the body of Bream was very useful for them. Although human's internal communications are much more complex they work according to the same principles that Cal and Phosphorus had encountered when they formed part of the fish. With the additional help of other atoms that were part of the shoulder blade, Cal and his thoughtful companion were quickly able to connect up to

Francisco's senses, through which they were once more able to see and listen to the world.

The first picture that they had of the outside world was that of some planks on the jetty. Of course they were hugely disappointed. They had got used to Bream's sight, which was imperfect, blurred and blotchy, just enough for the poor thing to avoid bumping into other fish or to spot some prey in the water. With such a model you would imagine that they expected something far superior from the sight of a human. I have to say that although they could see better than they could through the eyes of Bream, the two atoms were still restricted to seeing only a narrow band of the spectrum, from red to violet or violet to red, without being able to go beyond those arbitrary limits of Nature. Compared to the memories of what they could see (so to speak) as they travelled through space, or in the days when they were contemplating the enormity of the heavens, human vision seemed to them to be rather limited, which frankly disappointed them. Their atomic vision enabled them to enjoy the whole spectrum, without any absurd restrictions: the infinite riches of infra-red and ultraviolet radiation, the incredible power of X-rays, the symphony of the microwaves that fill stellar space. In short, the picture of the real world that Cal and Phosphorus could see when they were free was complete, it covered everything and they missed nothing, whereas the sight that they had through the eyes of a human was now basic and uncertain. They realized that Nature had given humans what was essential to survive in a hostile world and to achieve their basic objectives, but not much more than that. In fact human sight was very imperfect and narrow. The real world was so different and so much more beautiful!

After supper Juan and Francisco went out for a walk. After a while they sat down on the edge of the jetty, lit up a cigarette and let their gaze wander across to the nearby lighthouse and the small beach.

At such intimate moments Juan liked to talk seriously.

"Last Sunday I went to Joaquín's house. He's studying at the University of Oviedo."

"What's he studying?" asked Francisco.

"Math, but he told me that he wants to study astronomy."

"What's that?"

"Don't be dumb, Paquito, astronomy is the study of heavenly bodies. You study the sky, the stars, the planets... and how they move around in the heavens. Joaquín is passionate about it, he talks about nothing else. He told me that the stars we see are not the only ones there are, but only the ones that our sight enables us to see. And if we look at the sky with a telescope which is like a giant magnifying glass, we would see millions of them."

"Millions?"

"Yes, millions. What's more, when they know how to make more powerful telescopes we'll be able to see right into the depths of the sky and then we'll discover many more stars. And you know something else? Joaquín says that the Sun is also a star, that the stars that we can see are like other suns."

Excited by what Juan was telling him, Francisco swung his legs to and fro. He listened with growing interest.

"One of his Profs, Professor Hernández, thinks that many of those stars have planets, like the Sun has, and that it is highly likely that there is life on many of those planets, just like Earth."

They looked up at the sky. They had looked at it before, but never as they did on that night.

As his second cigarette went out in the sea, Francisco sat and thought for half a minute and then shook his head as if he didn't want to go on thinking. Juan guessed what he was about to do, stood up and offered him his hand. Together they started back. On one side of the jetty, in the distance, a flash of lightning warned of an impending storm.

The atoms, who had been listening to the conversation, were surprised by the brothers' naivety. If only they could explain to them! For example... that the Earth is a tiny dot lost in the Universe... that the Milky Way, with its four hundred thousand million stars, is only one among thousands of millions of galaxies just like it... that very many stars have planets.... that in a countless number of planets...

But no, it was impossible. The means of communication that they had established with Francisco's brain only worked in one direction: from him to them.

6

LIFE IN OTHER WORLDS

Nitrogen was an experienced atom. He formed part of a neuron of the shoulder blade, next to where Cal and Phosphorus were. Since he had been in Francisco's body for some time he felt obliged to advise the new arrivals:

"Listen, given where you are I wouldn't get your hopes up too much. You should know - although I imagine that you already do - that you'll remain set in the structure of that bone, in other words, you'll be stuck for some time. If you were in a different place, the removing cells might return you to the bloodstream in two or three months, but where you are in the shoulder blade, I doubt that very much. You'll have worked out already that you can receive information from Francisco's senses: seeing, listening, feeling movement, the heat and the cold, but I should warn you that you will also be able to get in touch with his memory. I recommend this for the time that you have ahead of you in captivity. It will doubtless be the activity that will bring you most comfort, since you'll get to know information that Francisco has stored from a past that will never repeat itself - from his emotions a moment ago to images of events that he experienced some time back. This knowledge will enable you to share the history of a boy as many times as you like, to dwell on every thought, on every memory, and if you are curious, I imagine you'll also be able to enjoy delving into his feelings."

In fact Cal could not hold back his curiosity:

"Can you connect us up right now with his brain, Nitrogen, so that we can get into his memory?"

Nitrogen agreed. As soon as they had done so they realized that Francisco's memory had an extraordinary capacity.

"Almost like ours!" said Phosphorus.

They were reasonable atoms and bearing in mind that it was a first experience they limited themselves to looking only for memories from the last twenty-four hours. It turned out to be quite easy. They quickly found the images they wanted, the ones that the death of Bream had prevented them from seeing. Looking into the memory of a young person is like having an HD recording: the memories are sharp and not blurred by the passage of time. It is therefore not surprising that recalling them is almost like reliving them.

Cal and Phosphorus saw clearly the scene in which Bream came out of the sea, the line that dragged him towards the boat and the moment when Francisco took out the hook. Soon they could see the entry into the harbour, the moment when Juan put them in the basket, the family scene when they got home, the exchanges with the mother, until finally they had a first view of the grill and the fire. That was when Cal muttered:

"That's why the water molecules abandoned us…"

The memory then showed them the crucial scene in which Francisco spiked the piece of fish and took it to his mouth, which enabled them to understand in detail what had happened to them, in other words, how they had managed to enter a human body. You might think that they would be moved by this information, but it wasn't like that, or rather not only like that. To be honest, they found the last scene so amusing that they decided to repeat it over and over again, and each time they found something new! Francisco's memory was indefatigable and vast, and they could go back and see each one of his memories as many times as they liked! No, Nitrogen had not been wrong.

At three in the morning a storm broke. The wind and the rain prevented Ricardo and his sons from going out fishing that morning. At twelve the temperature had dropped sufficiently for them all to feel like eating the bean stew that Carmen had prepared the night before. The family of fishermen ate almost in silence. For their part Cal and

Phosphorus expectantly looked at the sea through Francisco's eyes. First the waves that went over the jetty as if they were trying to take it with them, a bit further out the rough sea, and on one side the hill of Barrio Alto with its elegant houses that they saw for the first time.

After lunch Juan decided to visit Joaquín, as that afternoon his friend was going back to Oviedo. Francisco asked if he could go with him:

"I'd like to hear Joaquín tell one of those stories about astronomy."

Juan loved his brother very much, but his wacky idea drove him crazy. Reluctantly he agreed. What concern could this 'child' have with a conversation between grown men?

They left the house with waterproof capes over their heads and started up the hill towards Barrio Alto. Joaquín's family's house was one of the largest and nicest in the town. From its windows the sight of the Cantabrian Sea was stunning.

Joaquín was a thin boy, taller than Juan, with straight fair hair combed with a side parting and a stray lock that flopped over his forehead from time to time. A pair of rimless glasses with round lenses perched on his aquiline nose.

When they entered the room Joaquín seemed pleased to see Francisco and gave him a firm hug.

"Paquito, what a surprise! I wasn't expecting to see you today…. Wow, how you've grown, you're as big as a bear! Say, I've got to take the bus for Oviedo in a couple of hours, so we can chat while I put away my things."

As if apologizing for the presence of his brother, Juan said:

"Francisco wanted to come and see you because last night I was telling him your stories about astronomy and I left him half crazed. He wants you to explain it to him face-to-face; he's not very convinced by what I told him."

"No, it's not like that," said Francisco, "your explanations seemed fine. I understood everything, even that stuff about that telescope thing. What I can't get into my head is that up there on other planets there are people living like us."

"Look, Paquito," said Joaquín, "I believe what my Prof says. He says that in the Milky Way there are more than a million stars and that if we at least had the same luck as that guy who won the jackpot in the Christmas lottery there would be at least another hundred planets inhabited by beings like us. In fact he believes that there must be many more than a hundred inhabited planets. The thing is that they are so far from the Earth that we'll never be able to communicate with them."

"Tell me, Joaquín, did God also create all these other inhabited planets?"

Joaquín and Juan looked at each other. They were both agnostics and in those turbulent times of the Republic they belonged to a group of young socialists in the town.

"Why do you ask me that, Paquito? If, as you believe, God created everything, he must have made the stars and the planets. Or do you think that there's one God for the Earth and other gods for the other stars?"

"No, of course not," Francisco answered in some confusion, "but I must tell you something: I was thinking all night and I can't understand why God just chose to send Jesus Christ, his only son, to Earth. What did he do with the inhabitants of the other planets? How did He convince them to believe in Him? Because on those other planets the people will also be Catholics, won't they?"

Francisco's argument unsettled Joaquín, who didn't know what to say in reply. Paquito's ingenuousness was disturbing. He decided to avoid the question:

"I really respect your beliefs, although you know that your brother and I don't believe the same things as you do. But within your religion there must be some explanation for your doubts, a basic belief that I am not aware of. I think that it would be a good subject to discuss with the parish priest, Father Asdrúbal, after mass on Sunday."

Cal and Phosphorus had followed the conversation without understanding very much at all. They were particularly confused by the figure of the son of God.

"Cal, I think we'd better ask Nitrogen to connect us up to his memory again; I'm sure we'll find something that will explain things. God is quite like our Creator of the Universe, although it sounds as though He does other things as well. Be that as it may, the one I can't get is Jesus. It seems that he was a human being...."

"Phosphorus, don't go on about your idea of the Creator of the Universe; most of us atoms don't think that way. Besides, before getting connected with his memory to see if we can find anything, I would wait for Francisco's talk with Father Asdrúbal. Apparently he's someone who knows a lot and his explanation will probably make things clear for us."

It had stopped raining and Joaquín needed to get the bus for Oviedo. The brothers said goodbye to him, went down the hill and headed for the fishermen's neighbourhood.

In his room Francisco stretched out on his bed with his hands behind his head. The paint on the ceiling was peeling and there was a clear patch of damp in the corner. He was upset; they had treated him like a child and he felt himself to be a man. He had no arguments to put back to his know-it-all brother or Joaquín, who thought he possessed the absolute truth. He had asked them in good faith and he could still feel their replies like a blow to the pit of his stomach. He was not going to allow it to happen again. The best thing would be to talk to the priest; he would give him something to say to Juan and Joaquín that would leave them speechless. He pictured the scene... A smile came to his lips, the tension in his body evaporated, he closed his eyes and soon fell asleep.

Cal took advantage of the peace and quiet to think to himself...

'I'm almost a thousand million years old, I'm still young... I look at Phosphorus, aged five thousand million, and I don't see any great differences between us, except our disagreement about whether the Universe had a creator or not. Of course, he's got more experience, but I know more about some subjects that he doesn't know anything about. It's true that his nucleus is in good shape – there's no doubt about that – and his electrons still surround him energetically as well. I wonder if when I get to his age in about four thousand million years time, I'll have the same strength as he has...'

When he got to this point Cal shuddered. If he reached the age of Phosphorus he would witness the end of the Solar

System and with it the end of the Earth. He didn't want to think about that.

'Fate has led me to my present situation. My greatest wish was to enter a human body and I succeeded in doing so... What have I got to complain about? I must make the most of this opportunity. I have been chosen! Tomorrow I shall be one of the few atoms that has known human beings... If, as I assume, humans will live for a limited period and then disappear, just like the dinosaurs, I will have been part of an exceptional event.'

He looked to one side and saw Phosphorus, still imperturbable, in one of his lethargic moods that could last for weeks on end. Aware that he was different, Cal reached a conclusion that made him feel even more excited:

'Yes, I'm quite sure about it. I'll try to learn everything I can about them, and when I'm old, the most interesting stories that I'll tell the younger atoms will be about human beings, just as Hydrogen did with me.'

7

HUMAN FEELINGS

The following morning the storm was still raging and once again the fishing trip was cancelled. As happened every Thursday there was a meeting in the priest's house of young people receiving religious instruction. Francisco could hardly ever attend because of his work.

In the afternoon it stopped raining and so he decided to go up the hill along the narrow paved street, where the balconies were full of pink and red geraniums that stood out against the whiteness of the walls. The church and the priest's house looked out on to a small square facing the sea on the hill of the Barrio Alto.

The door of the priest's house was open. Francisco went down a long corridor which led to a room that served as dining room and study room, where the priest was with half a dozen boys between twelve and fifteen years old.

Father Asdrúbal greeted him with a nod of his head and indicated where he should sit.

"Let's go on with the class that we had started when Francisco arrived. As I said, today's subject is the story of John the Baptist."

Francisco interrupted him:

"Forgive me, Father, but something very important has come up and I would like you to explain it to me. I think it would be useful for the others here, too."

"Go on…"

"On the other planets of the Universe where there is life like ours, and there are more than a hundred of them, I want to know what God did to save their inhabitants if he couldn't send Jesus. And I would also like you to explain if Purgatory and Hell are the same for all the inhabited planets in the Universe or if each one has its own."

"Who's the fool who has put such lies into your head?… Francisco, how many times have I told you that your friendship with that communist Joaquín López could do you great harm, especially in the times that we're living in. These atheists don't know what to come up with next. I insist that you stop seeing him. If you promise me that, I will say nothing about this to your mother, and what's more I will explain to you everything you want to know about the planets."

"The thing is, Father, Joaquín's a close friend of my brother Juan. And he's not a communist, Father, he's a socialist."

"Your brother is another one who has strayed. He hasn't been to church for a long time. And let's have no more of your 'he's not a communist'. All of them, I'll have you know, all of them are reds and enemies of Spain!... Francisco, I haven't yet heard your promise."

"I promise I'll do my best not to see him, Father. Or maybe I'll see him just once more in order to rub his face in what you're going to tell me about the planets."

A long pause hung over the room. Then Father Asdrúbal said:

"Let's consider the little story that Francisco brought us, about men who could be living on other planets. If there's one thing clear from Genesis, which we studied last year, it is that God created men on Earth and not in other parts of the Universe. Remember this verse: 'Thus the heaven and the earth were finished, and all the host of them'. The word 'Earth'," he stressed, "is repeated several times in Genesis so that we are in no doubt, and besides there is never any mention of the stars as a place for life. In any case the only planets that exist are those that we know in our Solar System, for no astronomer has discovered any others. So that's enough of that nonsense. What I have told you is the word of God."

And with that he considered the matter closed.

"Now let's go on with John the Baptist"

The atoms looked at each other in astonishment; they couldn't believe it. Cal just managed to say:

"If only we could tell them the truth…"

During supper Francisco didn't mention anything to Juan about the meeting in the priest's house. They spoke about other matters, especially the political situation. The left-wing government that was in power in Spain was going through a critical situation that was difficult to sustain. Every day there were demonstrations and political rallies.

In the dark night the stars were shining more brightly than usual. Francisco went out into the yard, looked up and was lost in contemplation of them. After a while he fetched his waterproof cape and lay down on it. First he stared on one star, then on the one next to it, and so on one by one until he fixed his gaze on the brightest star. Again and again he imagined that a planet just like Earth was going round and round it, and he stayed like that without moving for a whole hour. Then he slowly got up and dragging his cape behind him he went back into the house.

Days later, one morning in July 1936, when Francisco was getting ready to have breakfast, news of the uprising of the Military Union shook the Fishermen's Quarter. The Civil War had started. The whole of that region of Spain stayed under the control of the Republican Government. Every town organized its militia to face the revolution, and Juan and Joaquín enlisted in it at once. It was now three years since Cal became part of Francisco's shoulder-blade.

The company that the Republicans had recruited in the town was assigned to cover an area to the south of Gijón, with the aim of blocking a secondary route through which it was assumed that part of the Army, which was assembled in Oviedo, would attempt to advance northwards.

One night after supper they received the order to get ready to leave the next morning.

The two friends were just about to go to bed when they saw Francisco's head appear round the barracks' door.

"Nice of you to come and say goodbye!" exclaimed Joaquín.

A small bag hung from Francisco's right shoulder.

"I haven't come to say goodbye, I'm coming with you."

Juan suddenly went crazy.

"Don't talk nonsense, Paquito! You've no military training and you're too young."

"I'll run errands, work in the kitchen, anything, whatever I can do."

Phosphorus and Cal were listening carefully and getting ready to go through the experience. Cal, in particular, took in every detail and imagined himself in his old age telling the story to the amazement of the gathering of atoms.

A little while later the two militiamen were fast asleep, worn out by the chores of the day. Francisco, by contrast, couldn't get to sleep. He found the camp bed very hard and the barracks uncongenial. He just couldn't settle. Different scenes went through his mind until the face of Beatriz appeared and he became less tense. He had met her a few months earlier at the meetings in the priest's house and after a few days they had sworn everlasting love. He told her: 'Beatriz, I love you so much, you make me feel so happy!' She replied: 'I love you too, Paquito, but don't squeeze me so tight – I don't like it.' 'It's only for a short time; I'm going off to war and I may get killed and we would never see each other again.' Then Beatriz shuddered and let Paquito hold her as tight as he liked.

The two atoms were quite amused by the situation.

Phosphorus said:

"I'm sure she likes it, too."

This was a completely new subject and so the discussion kept them occupied for several hours. Suddenly the sensations received via Francisco's feelings aroused in Phosphorus a desire to talk that he had never had before. There was no concept equivalent to human love amongst the atoms; the closest was the attraction that kept them joined together in the phosphate molecule. That's what Cal thought, and to illustrate it he recalled at length the relationship that he had had with Oxygen in that exchange of electrons and the formation of calcium oxide. Phosphorus and Cal considered these comparisons, but what was happening to Francisco with Beatriz was quite different. Would they manage to understand it?

"I told you, given the way in which they are getting together it's like the attraction between us."

"No," replied Phosphorus, "you're thinking of your particular case and what happened to you with Oxygen as just two atoms. But in my youth, in the molecule in which I travelled towards the Sun, there were nine of us!"

"Then it must be what Nitrogen told me the other day, I almost forgot! You were off on one of your lethargic spells and so you didn't hear about it. He explained that human beings feel something called 'sexual attraction'. According to Nitrogen it's very enjoyable and it's nothing like our atomic experiences."

While Cal and Phosphorus were having this discussion Francisco was picturing himself and Beatriz caressing each other for a long time. This thought had a soothing effect on his nerves. And while the atoms gave free rein to their discussion, he at last managed to fall asleep.

8

THE TRENCH

For over a hundred kilometers several dilapidated trucks ferried the company to its destination. Many locals, with carts loaded with their possessions, tried to get away from the combat zone and blocked the road. Cal found everything as interesting as he had when he discovered the first amino acid swimming alongside him in the ocean.

The militiamen dug trenches on a small hill. Further back in the valley they pitched the tents. Every so often loud explosions broke the murmuring and the silence: the mine workers from Asturias who were experts with explosives blew up bridges and sewers to impede the enemy's advance. Large blocks of stone were rolled on the road and a small tractor with a front shovel pushed them to make barricades.

After four days of preparations, some enemy reconnaissance planes flew overhead at dawn. Down in their trench Joaquín and the two brothers were having ham and cheese rolls for breakfast and talking, just like the good times. Their favourite topics were the usual ones, but the dialectic fight was very unequal. Francisco put forward his highly dogmatic arguments, but ones which he doubtless believed, while the two older ones ranged their discourse against him. Although theirs was rational, it still had a whiff of sectarianism about it which had been learnt on some socialist indoctrination courses.

Joaquín and Juan, who crushed Francisco with their arguments, hadn't given up hope of converting him. In the most recent discussion on life on other planets they had noticed that he had rather changed his views.

Cal and Phosphorus found these discussions a very useful means of getting to know humans better and so they tried not to miss a word. Amongst the new terms the ones that most aroused their curiosity were 'fascism' and 'socialism' and amongst the topics there was one that intrigued Phosphorus more than it did Cal: German aviation. By contrast they were troubled by the ignorance that the young men displayed about the real Universe. If they could have done so they would have liked to tell them the truth. However, they felt that such a revelation would in any case be inopportune, since – they reckoned – only the passage of time, which could even be hundreds of years, would slowly reveal the mystery of their existence to human beings.

The air seemed to be electrified by the imminence of battle. In the trenches, which scored the hillside like knife marks, fear and courage represented opposing means by which to escape from reality. Almost all of the militiamen were very young, novices in the activities of war. They were overrun by the advance of an organized army, which had the support of German and Italian planes.

Francisco shouted angrily at his companions:

"You crack jokes in order to hide your fear... I'd like to see you when they attack us. At the first sound of gunfire you'll all run off!"

"I shan't run off," Joaquín replied.

"Then you'll have to kill – which I doubt you'll dare to do - or be killed. If you kill, you must know that it's a mortal sin. And as you're a hopeless atheist no-one will forgive you your sin and so you'll go straight to Hell. You can forget about Purgatory!"

Cal and Phosphorus, who were bound to the shoulder blade, and Nitrogen, in the next-door neuron, were following the conversation closely. Cal was confused by the word 'sin'.

"What does 'sin' mean?"

"First you'll have to understand what religion is," Nitrogen replied.

"Religion?" said Phosphorus, confused.

"We'd better just listen..." Cal was bubbling over with curiosity.

"Calm down, Francisco," said Joaquín. "I don't believe in Hell or Purgatory or Paradise and I'm not at all afraid of death because I believe I know what it means. I don't know what I'll feel when I die but I do know that *I* shall never be dead because when death comes, at that very moment *I* shall have ceased to exist."

Francisco was indignant:

"Don't talk nonsense, Joaquín. So you think that you'll die and that'll be that?"

"Yes, that's what I think, but what I want now is for you to get rid of your fear and to think a bit, or can't you see that you're suffering because you're afraid of the unknown? And of all the things that are unknown, the one that worries you most is the most unfathomable one: death."

"You're too clever by half, Joaquín. Here we are, the two of us waiting for them to attack us and to calm our nerves the best idea you can come up with is to give me a lesson in philosophy. Don't you think it would be better if we talked about how to get out of this trench? I'm suffocating."

Cal thought out loud:

"None of the three of them understands what death is."

"Don't you believe it," retorted Phosphorus. "Joaquín does. For him it has the same meaning as the end does for us:

the loss of identity. What happens is that people live for a very short time and can't stand the idea that one day they'll cease to exist."

"When my existence comes to an end I'll be transformed into energy…" said Nitrogen hopefully.

"In order to form my nucleus ten helium nuclei joined together and ceased to exist," Cal explained nostalgically.

"I think I'll exist for ever," Phosphorus concluded.

At that moment a distant droning became a deafening noise within a matter of seconds. Dozens of planes were approaching from the south. The aircraft passed straight over the trenches and attacked the artillery set up behind them. Having blown up almost all of the cannons and artillerymen of the Republican forces, the planes passed over the young men once more in the opposite direction as they returned to their bases. Joaquín took the initiative.

"Juan, get going and take Francisco with you. You've got to save him. They're going to destroy us all here!"

A second wave of planes approached. Francisco wept, unable to speak. Then Juan gave him a shove and got him out of the trench that was protecting them.

"Run along the slope towards those trees! Can you see them? I'll be right with you."

Paquito hesitated and then ran like a man possessed. After two hundred meters he tripped on a root, rolled along the ground and could only cover his eyes with his hands.

Cal and Phosphorus were disturbed by the running and the blow but couldn't see what was happening. They turned to Nitrogen:

"I can't see anything, either, but you can't imagine what Francisco's nervous system is like. I'm getting some very strange signals constantly going back and forth through my neuron. Has he gone mad?"

The same idea suddenly occurred to the three atoms: was Francisco going to die in combat? That would condemn Cal and Phosphorus to remain motionless in this wretched bone, maybe for centuries. The only one who could save himself in a short period of time was Nitrogen.

Back in the trenches the first planes were merciless: while the soldiers could neither escape nor respond to the attack, the machine-guns fired in relentless bursts. The first one to die was Joaquín. He wasn't able to fire a single shot. He couldn't wound or kill anyone. It wasn't necessary for God to forgive him his sin.

A cloud of dust covered the trenches and left them hidden. The few survivors, with Juan amongst them, ran down towards the wood. One of them shouted:

"The enemy's armoured cars are coming – they're about three hundred meters away!"

When Juan got to the small wood the brothers hugged each other. Francisco knew what his older brother was going to say:

"Leave him," he said. "If death is as you believe, Joaquín no longer exists. Forget about his body – it's no longer *him*."

Juan led the march northwards, followed by the whole group. He wanted to get to the west of Gijón to find out if they could get back to their home town, either along the shore or by sea. No-one knew for certain where the enemy was making its advance; all they could be sure of was that they were being pursued by a column from the south. Deep down Francisco was growing anxious and his heart was pounding from the effort and the anguish that was gripping him like a giant fist. The atoms were filled with despair and were afraid that soon a bullet would finish him off, just like Joaquín. Would they have better luck? Would Hydrogen's prediction come true?

Cal wanted to look at the road, but the image was blurred: he couldn't see because of Francisco's tears.

At the coast the group split up. While the majority headed for Gijón, Francisco and his brother managed to climb into a small truck that was heading west towards their home town. Along the line of vehicles the rumour was spreading that very close by the enemy advance parties that were trying to surround Gijón with a pincer movement would soon catch up with them. Without hesitation the two militiamen jumped down and ran for the coast. From an isolated house that seemed to hang from the hillside they could hear the radio broadcasting the latest news of the war. The owner listened in astonishment to Juan's request:

"Ma'am, if you can shelter us until nightfall we'll try to escape. We won't give you any trouble."

"Come in quickly and shut the door."

Juan accepted a bite to eat and Francisco lay down to rest. When he closed his eyes, Cal and his friends could no longer view the outside world but could clearly see the idealized figure of Beatriz: the girl's gaze was bolder than it was in real life. Francisco thought about her kisses for some time. Then, contented, he fell asleep.

At that precise moment Cal recalled Hydrogen's advice. If Francisco died his fate and that of Phosphorus would be terrible. How many centuries would they spend under the earth?

When night fell the good woman said goodbye and gave the two brothers lots of suggestions. She advised them to head for the coast where fishing boats were taking militia men to Gijón. The trees and plants on the slope down to the sea would give them cover.

Once there they thought they could see in the semi-darkness one of the boats trying to get to the coast. Juan calculated the risks and told Paquito to run to the shore.

"I'll cover you from here. When you feel safe give me a signal and I'll come down to join you."

Two gun shots cracked through the air. Francisco seemed to take off and fell on to the sand very close to the water's edge. The attackers, who were wearing the three-cornered hats of the Civil Guard, celebrated their good shots by roaring with laughter. One of the bullets went through his back, deflected on to the shoulder-blade and went out through his chest.

The piece of lead travelled the few meters that separated Francisco from the shore and fell into the sea. The impact had shattered the bone into pieces. Nitrogen saw Cal and Phosphorus disappear from his side and there was blood everywhere. Swept along by the bullet, the two friends were left on a tiny splinter together with thousands of other calcium phosphate molecules.

During the flight which had lasted about a second they were accompanied by a drop of blood. When they came into contact with the water, Cal had the clear sensation of returning to the past, to the time of his freedom, when he dived towards the depths or prowled near the surface to be caressed by the light. Nitrogen was no longer with them. Although he was somewhat upset by this, what saddened him most was the realization that Nitrogen had not got to know what the sea was like…

Once they had recovered from their immediate impression Cal and Phosphorus tried to escape from the embrace of the other atoms that formed the splinter with them, but they were in for a major surprise: despite the efforts of the water molecules which flowed among the grains of sand in order to take them with them, they couldn't get away. Then a bromide ion, who like all bromides was ready to give his opinion, said:

"I don't think you can escape. The calcium phosphate molecule that you are combined in is virtually insoluble in water. The most likely thing is that you'll stay bound to this bit of bone splinter for many more years."

Phosphorus seemed resigned and buried himself in his thoughts. Not Cal, however, who was always hopeful that things would change. He had had the enormous good fortune to be one of the few who had managed to escape from Francisco's body... he was not now going to be buried in the sand!

Five months later near the shore the waves stirred the bottom of the sea, moving Cal and Phosphorus to and fro. By this time the friction against the grains of sand had broken up the bone splinter and it was on the point of turning to dust. On the surface of one of its particles, Cal fought tirelessly, for he was being tugged hard this way and that: on one hand the water molecules that were dragging him strongly towards them, and on the other hand the calcium phosphate molecules that were trying to keep him in the solid structure of the splinter. The water finally won and the calcium phosphate molecule dissolved. In short, our friends were transformed: Cal lost two of his electrons and became an ion again. For his part Phosphorus, who was bound to three oxygen atoms (his companions in the molecule), was also free and now formed part of a phosphate ion.

Just as Cal tried to say something to him a wave breaking on the beach mixed water with sand and caused him to turn over and over as if in a small whirlwind. He didn't want to miss saying goodbye to Phosphorus but although he looked for him everywhere he didn't manage to see him again. After all, amongst atoms these sudden farewells are very common.

9

A REVEALING MEMORY

Back in the Cantabrian Sea once again, Cal enjoyed his freedom more than he could ever remember having done before. He spent some unforgettable years there, while the sea currents kept him close to the coast, which varied from rocky cliffs, to slopes of lush vegetation and extensive beaches with golden sands. You could say that at that time Cal was on an extended holiday. His greatest fun was to join the foam that formed on the crest of the waves: a very thin layer of water molecules and ions that surrounded tiny little pockets of air, which couldn't escape from their captivity and turned into millions of bubbles. The magic only lasted for seconds and then the bubble burst and Cal was shot out through the air and fell back down again. Sometimes he reached the shore, he mingled with the sand and was rescued by the next wave. On other occasions he had to wait for hours until the Moon caused the next high tide. As you can imagine Cal was happy with his new life.

One afternoon in 1941, a little more than five years since his return to the sea, the current brought him towards a small port which he recognized: the side of a hill covered in white houses, a church tower and by the wooden jetty a long line of fishing boats. The shape of the lighthouse finally convinced him: the last time he had seen that view was the day when, bound to Francisco's shoulder-blade, he left the town being shaken around in the back of an old truck. Cal spent the night remembering being confined in Francisco's shoulder-blade, Phosphorus' unexpected absences and the constant willingness of Nitrogen to connect them to the outside world. What strange years, he thought, like someone thinking about a weekend, how difficult they were and how different, too…

Early in the morning the fishermen started their daily routine. As they set sail the boats split up into groups of three which went in different directions. Cal noticed one group slowly heading towards him. In the leading boat the captain was leaning over the rail and a curly head of hair appeared from under his cap.

A strange sensation went through our atom. Could it be that Francisco had escaped death? Cal felt moved and wondered whether Nitrogen might be with him. As he went past, the captain unbuttoned his trousers, looked at the slight swell of the sea and began to urinate. Some drops of urine were blown by the wind and fell beside Cal, mixing with the water. Thousands of ions landed around him! Dying of curiosity, he rushed over to one of them, a calcium ion no less, and asked him anxiously:

"That man is Francisco, isn't he? Are you part of him?"

The other calcium looked at him in disbelief, as if he had bumped into a ghost ion.

"How do you know his name?"

"I was part of Francisco. I left him five years ago. It was on a beach, when he was shot in the back. I thought he had died."

Cal has his work cut out convincing his fellow ion of this experience. He had to tell him a lot of private details about Francisco before the other one would believe him. Sure enough, it was him. As the boat sailed into the distance and grew smaller, the other calcium explained that he had arrived in Francisco's body shortly before he set off for the war in a tonic that his mother made him drink every morning to strengthen his bones.

"How ironical," he added. "The tonic was to strengthen his bones and I didn't end up in any of them. I stayed in his blood all this time!"

Cal was keen to know what had happened to Francisco after he and Phosphorus were swept into the sea.

"It was all very confusing," the other calcium explained. "As I was travelling around his body I knew that Francisco was not dead. In my travels I never went near the wound; if I had, I too would have ended up on the sand. I couldn't see anything of the outside world because he had his eyes closed, but then I heard Juan's voice and later the voices of other people. The attackers had given him up for dead, so they went away. Juan asked for help from some people in a boat that was just offshore and between them they put him on board and took him to Gijón. Two or three days later when Francisco finally opened his eyes, the first image that I saw was that of a woman dressed in white who was looking at him with great happiness."

He was a very pleasant ion and had a prodigious memory. We know how inquisitive and communicative Cal is, so it's not surprising that they became good friends. The truth is that they had good reason to be; their common memories helped to consolidate their affection and after a while they even started to call each other 'brother'.

Their friendship lasted for about twenty years, until the day they decided to swim in the bottom of the sea. They loved to be amongst those strange fish that were able to endure the enormous pressure of the depths. They said to each other:

"We atoms are not affected by the pressure of the water, but it must do something to those poor creatures... Look at that one's strange shape!"

That afternoon, while they were dazzled by the skill of a star fish capturing its prey, they didn't notice the crowd of small crustaceans approaching. When Cal saw them his memory took him back hundreds of millions of years and he remembered Magnesium, the companion he used to go around with, when he was taken in by one of those little creatures. He turned round to alert his brother to the danger, but it was too late. He then saw him disappear into one of those little bodies, with a mixture of fear and curiosity, like a child looking through the display cabinets in a natural science museum. Cal remained next to the crustacean for a long time. Many water molecules and numerous ions reappeared, but not his brother.

During the following months he continued to wait for him. He looked at the shells of all the little creatures that he came across... they were full of calcium atoms! There were millions of them; how was he going to find his friend amongst them? He supposed that he wouldn't be captive for long; a fish had probably swallowed him and at any moment, give or take a millennium, he would reappear.

During the decades that followed Cal made many new friends, whom he entertained with his stories about human beings. None of them had known them as closely as he had, so he always amused and surprised the other atoms with his interesting details.

It was towards the end of July 1998, which is summer in Spain. Sixty years had passed since his return to the sea. The north winds had always kept him close to the Asturian coast. From his observatory on the crest of a wave Cal could study the golden sands of the Aguilar beach, the mouth of the stream that divides it in two and on one side several caves or grottoes carved out by the pounding of the water on the rocks of the cliffs. The best known was the Palacio de la Cueva and next to it the rocky outcrop of El Carballar (according to the legend this was a knight turned to stone who, on certain occasions, flies the flag of Asturias as if it were nailed to the top of it).

The periods opposite the beach were the best for watching the bathers with their attractive costumes and the multi-coloured sunshades planted in the sand like giant pins. But since the bullet wound that had returned him to the sea in 1936, Cal had kept his promise, so to speak, not to allow any fish or human being to capture him again. To achieve this he had used all his ingenuity, with the conviction that the best course of action was to let himself be carried along by the thermal currents near the surface. The fish rarely came up that far and when they did it was to try to catch some insect trapped by the water.

In spite of this strong fear of being captured, and without really understanding why, often when he remembered Francisco's body he pictured a palace, he thought about his adventures and he considered himself to be his accomplice.

So far I have insisted that atoms are sufficiently different from humans so as not to be mistaken for them. But I have to acknowledge that, at that particular time in his existence, Cal was behaving rather like a human being, or at least he was for a few moments. Imagine him asking himself… Why not have a similar experience again? Maybe the fact that he had formed part of a human had left a mark on him in that sense. We just don't know. On the other hand it is also true that his days in the sea were repeating themselves over and over again, and sometimes Cal even felt that they only changed for the worse. He let himself to be swept along by life in the sea, where the only new thing, as far as an atom was concerned, consisted in modifying a small detail one year, another one the following year, such that in the end nothing changed and everything carried on as before. How long will I go on like this? he asked himself. Of course he didn't always feel fed up, but around 1998 his boredom had grown to the point where he found it almost unbearable. Yes, Cal was in crisis.

It's not difficult to conclude that if the possibility of entering a human being is minimal for an atom, the possibility of entering for a second time is almost zero. But what was there to lose by trying it?

When he asked himself, Cal invariably remembered the advice of Hydrogen:

"Son," the wise old timer had said to him in an affectionate way, "you have more than a ninety per cent chance of ending up in one of the bones, and, if you don't manage to escape from there, a little while later you'll end up in a grave, where you will remain buried for centuries as if you were part of dolomite."

It's strange – although Cal had always listened carefully to Hydrogen, he had never thought about dolomite. He knew that it was a mineral consisting of calcium carbonate and magnesium that was found in the mountains, but that's all. Until that moment he had not stopped to consider fully how a calcium atom bound to a mineral must feel, and although it is true that such a fate seemed tragic, perhaps it wasn't. He had put up with the restrictions of being in a bone and in a shoulder-blade, and he thought that these calcium atoms had also accepted their fate and weren't suffering: they had decided to freeze time or perhaps time had agreed to sleep with them. Because if nothing changes, if everything is still, what is the meaning of time? Cal had never thought about this before. When he was young he had been taught that time measured the succession of moments that inexorably came and went. But things had to be different for the calcium atoms in dolomite: nothing happened to them… or perhaps it did?

Why had Hydrogen been so negative about his fate in the body of a human? He gave a lot of thought to Hydrogen's doubts, but in the end didn't think they were important. Often advice from old timers stems from a profound world-weariness, or perhaps a sense of frustration that they were unable to overcome during the course of their life. Their advice can therefore seem like a grievance. How can we know the truth? Maybe what Hydrogen felt was envy? Was he suffering because he himself hadn't managed to get into a human body?

And so, while he was watching the spectacle of the bathers on Aguilar beach, Cal's thoughts wandered between the advice of Hydrogen, dolomite and the meaning of time, until suddenly, without any warning from his memory, he remembered something that his brother (the calcium ion) had told him and to which he hadn't attached much importance. How strange memories are! Why do they suddenly appear like that? Who calls them up? Years had gone by since that conversation and now it reappeared, clear, pure, as if it had occurred yesterday.

The memory referred specifically to a conversation that Francisco and his mother had one Sunday in winter. With a bottle in one hand and a spoon in the other she begged her son:

"Francisco, you're a growing child, please, have some of this tonic. It's got calcium in it, which you need to give you strong bones now that you're growing up."

"It's got a nasty taste. You're going to make me throw up," was Francisco's reply.

"Don't be a silly boy, drink it," and she passed him a glass. "Take a spoonful and wash it down with some milk - you won't even taste it."

Francisco would have none of it. His mother insisted.

"You know what'll happen to you? You'll end up a feeble old man. It's important to take a lot of calcium because now you'll absorb all of it and it'll go straight into your bones. But when you're old you'll lose the calcium. If you don't believe me, just look at what happened to your poor grandmother Josefa: she broke her leg about three months ago and her bones don't want to mend. She'll be lame for the rest of her life."

The tussle between mother and son remained fresh in his atomic memory, but although Cal couldn't remember the end of the story, the message was very clear: it's unlikely that calcium gets into the bones of the elderly, since they lose more than they can retain.

Our atom turned his gaze once more to the bathers who were trying either to jump the waves or go underneath them. Many succeeded, but some lost their balance and were knocked over. They opened their mouth to breathe but all they got was water; they couldn't help swallowing it, then coughed and swallowed some more.

The strategy was simple and encouraged him to take action.

After a week the plan was ready. He would choose a day when the sea was rough so that there would be a greater number of people being knocked over. He would choose from among the bathers a man or a woman at least sixty years old and launch himself towards his objective by taking advantage of the breaker. The most difficult thing would be to enter the subject's mouth when they were trying to take in air, but then the worst bit would come: crossing his fingers so that their body would absorb him and cross them again so that he could stay in their bloodstream. He had to choose his prey and the opportunity carefully and not rush it, because he ran the risk of ruining the whole plan. Anyway, he had plenty of time. There were many days ahead when the beach would be full of people. It was only just about mid-summer.

10

THE RETURN

Roberto Alberdi was driving his four-door SEAT along the A66 motorway that runs between the cities of León and Oviedo. He was with his wife, who was dozing, safely strapped in by her seat-belt. Travelling by car was like taking a sleeping pill for Elvira.

He was sixty-three, tall and thin, with a broad forehead, green eyes and an open expression. Elvira was three years younger, slender and with fine features, her large warm eyes bright against her dark complexion. They had planned to spend a few days in Asturias, where Roberto's parents were from, which they were visiting for the first time.

They reached Oviedo after nightfall and arrived at the Hotel de la República where they would be spending the week. Early the next morning they went out to visit the beaches of the Cantabrian Sea. The concierge at the hotel had suggested they visit Aguilar beach. They took the motorway between Oviedo and Gijón and before they got to the port they turned left towards Avilés. They continued along a mountain road that runs parallel with the sea until they got to Muros del Nalón. From there they turned north along a very narrow lane overhung with trees and plants until suddenly, as if someone had drawn back a curtain, a long beach with golden sand appeared before them.

They stopped for a moment to look at the water, which was a deep blue sprinkled with small patches of black from the shadows of the clouds. The mouth of the Aguilar stream cut the beach in two and on one of its banks rose, bold and erect, the rocky outcrop of El Carballar. The waves, crowned by a crest of the whitest foam, broke ceaselessly on the shore.

They looked for a spot where they could spend the day. Several bar-restaurants, offering sunshades and deck chairs, vied for their custom. Elvira chose the one that looked most welcoming.

Meanwhile on the surface of the sea Cal decided that the moment had arrived to enter the body of a human being for a second time. He was determined to put into effect his plan of action; he had defined his tactics thanks to remembering his brother ion's anecdote.

The warning flag indicated that the sea was very rough, and this was clear from the power with which the waves were breaking. But Roberto was feeling hot and despite the warning he quickly went to the water's edge, took four or five strides and just as he did in his youth he plunged headfirst into the cold water. He swam out a few strokes but when he went to put his feet down the bottom of the sea had disappeared. He was in a dip, that broad, deep space that confuses the swimmer. He swam a few strokes and then a few more until the full force of a wave broke over him. Roberto couldn't stand up; he tried to breathe and swallowed water. The ebb and flow of the waves had brought Cal close to his target. He estimated his age and thought that here was the opportunity that he had longed for. He came back with the next wave at the very moment that Roberto tried to take in some air but only found water – enough for Cal to enter his mouth.

Two lifesavers who were looking on ran to help him, but before they could rescue him Robert's feet had landed on firm sand. After some advice and two or three slaps on the back, the life guards went back to their observation post.

Slowly Roberto headed back to the sunshade where Elvira, who was engrossed in the novel she was reading, remained unaware of the incident. He dropped down into the deckchair to recover from his ordeal.

Ever since he managed to enter Roberto's body Cal applied himself to carrying out his plan. First he had to get him to absorb him and not send him back into the sea. Then he had to stay in his bloodstream. He was definitely worried by the memory of his passage through Francisco's shoulder blade. But what he went through in Paquito's stomach and intestines was not going to be repeated: this time he had entered as an ion, he wasn't in a fish bone that had to be dissolved and no-one would attack him. It was later, when he got into the blood, that he would have to be careful...

Half an hour later Roberto suggested to Elvira that they go for a walk along the beach. They went quite a way along the sand, going at her lively pace, as far as the terrace of the Naútico restaurant. Later they had a well-chilled bottle of Marqués de Cáceres and a hake stew to share. By that time the tumble in the sea had been forgotten. When signs of the wine reached the intestines where Cal and his friends were waiting to be absorbed, a carbon atom that formed part of one of its molecules of alcohol - and who felt he had to say something - told Cal what was happening at the restaurant. We don't know whether he did so with the intention of worrying him – the carbon atoms of alcohol molecules are dreadful – or if it was just by chance. In any event this was what he said:

"They're talking about calcium."

Cal looked at him in surprise:

"How do they know I'm here?"

"No, they don't mean *you*. They mean calcium atoms *like* you. The woman says that when she gets back from their trip she's going to have her bone density measured.

"What's that?"

"According to what she's saying to her husband, it seems that they're going to put her in a machine to measure the percentage of minerals, in other words the percentage of you, that she has in her bones. She says that if the result isn't good the doctor will most likely prescribe calcium citrate for her and she mustn't forget to take it. The more of you she has in her body the stronger her bones will be."

Cal felt important - why not admit it? - although every time he heard the word 'bone' he started to tremble.

At four in the afternoon Roberto and Elvira agreed that it was time to go back to Oviedo. While they were driving along the motorway, retracing the route they had taken that morning, our atom was feeling very dizzy. Some water molecules were sliding along the wall of the intestine while others, Cal amongst them, were going through it. It took seconds but seemed like centuries. He had no doubts: it was time to take action.

He felt himself enter the red, turbulent bloodstream. Then he progressed along an artery, propelled by the piston thrusts of Roberto's heart at one beat per second. If he entered a smaller artery and then a smaller one still, he would be carried along by the lymph to his inevitable fate: he would be absorbed by one of the body's cells. In order to avoid it he had to stay in a main artery, place himself in the middle of the bloodstream and avoid bifurcations and secondary arteries. In the end his determination and his courage paid off; he avoided the risk of being absorbed and managed to remain in the bloodstream.

That is how Cal got to know the heart and lungs of his host, Roberto Alberdi.

11

AN INCREDIBLE DREAM

He enjoyed untold freedom. In the first few days Cal spent all his time going around Roberto's body, which was huge for something the size of an atom. Every time he was pumped around by his heart he hadn't any idea where he would end up and he enjoyed himself getting to know new places: a toe on one of his tours, flowing through a forearm on the next trip... Going through the lungs, where the red blood cells went to be oxygenated, was essential. Every tour took about ten minutes, so in just a few days he was able to visit almost the entire body.

The first time that the bloodstream took him to the brain he got very excited: the folds of the cortex seemed like castles and he was fascinated by the neurons. He remembered very clearly the one on Francisco's shoulder blade, where Nitrogen lived, but he never imagined that he was going to meet so many of them. The neurons were the most wonderful cells in the human body!

Five days after entering Roberto's body Cal got to see the outside world again through his eyes. The car was going along a mountain road full of hills with countless bends covered in abundant vegetation. Roberto was looking for the town of Pola de Siero, where his father had been born. Elvira, with map in hand, was helping him in the search. His father had died when Roberto was a child but he remembered vividly the stories his father had told him about his childhood. Roberto's memories were now mixed with images of the narrow street with the worn-out cobbles, the square without a name, in a familiar timeless scene.

While this was happening Cal realized that he was entering the brain again. So he decided to come away from Roberto's vision in order to explore where he liked. He was going along an artery, very close to its wall, when without knowing how or why he found himself in one of its cells. He entered it through a tiny channel and stopped. He was taken aback; was he going to be stuck again like he had been in Francisco's shoulder blade? Next to him a nitrogen atom who had noticed his anxiety said:

"Don't be afraid, calcium ions like you often visit us. Don't ask me who decides that you're going to enter our cell, because frankly I haven't a clue, but I can assure you that you will leave by exactly the same route as you came in and you'll go back to moving again. The human body uses you all to control its blood pressure."

Cal gave this some thought.

"Hey," said the nitrogen atom, "we'll be together for quite some time. How about if we take the opportunity to talk about the human brain?"

"I think that's an excellent idea," Cal replied. "I find it fascinating."

"What amazes me is how complex it is. What do you think of thoughts?"

"They're very different from ours."

"No, I don't mean what humans think about, but how their thoughts are formed."

"I don't know," said Cal, "I don't think they know how to explain it, either. They're only just starting to understand how their mind works."

"Some time ago we noticed with some other atoms how Roberto's brain works," he started to tell him. "We have a ringside seat in this artery. The brain grew according to the genetic code that Roberto inherited from his parents and later it ended up being molded by his lifetime experiences. We think that the functioning of the mind is conditioned and doesn't have the freedom that most humans attribute to it. That's why I asked you what you thought about it, since you've just encountered it. Another thing that we've noticed is that part of the brain is dedicated exclusively to planning for a future action, and to do this it carries out a large number of calculations in a fraction of a second. But Roberto is not aware of all this activity, only the result – in other words, what he has decided."

"And what is the implication of all this?" Cal asked, more curious than ever.

"My conclusion - and that of the other atoms who are interested in this - is that the type of computer that is the brain considers itself to have free will, but in reality that freedom does not exist. I could almost prove it to you. The true cause of a decision taken by Roberto can be very simple (for example, he burns himself and takes his hand away) or extremely complicated, when it appears chaotic. But that complexity does not stop his decision from being determined by an almost infinite number of causal connections."

"Is that what makes him think that he has been free to decide?"

"Of course, because the result of that mental process, which ends as his decision, was for him unpredictable."

"I think you're right," said Cal.

At that point in the conversation the tiny channel of the cell wall that had imprisoned him suddenly opened up. The water molecules and other ions of the blood took the opportunity to let him out. Although he presumed that he would not see the nitrogen atom again, he took his leave with "see you soon". After all, there are laws that operate in the blood and they have their raison d'être: with the number of small arteries that irrigate the brain it was fairly unlikely that he would return to the same place.

Well, Cal was moving along a vein that was so narrow that the red blood cells had to go in single file. The little vein must have had the same diameter as a blood cell. Cal and thousands of others like him, surrounded by water molecules, noted that Roberto's blood pressure had returned to normal when they came out into a larger vein. This vein in turn connected to another larger one, whose normal path led them to take in some oxygen in a lung.

Just as he and Phosphorus had enjoyed their visits to Francisco's memory, Cal was fascinated by Roberto's memory. Or rather he was even more excited because at the age of sixty Roberto had stored an incredible number of memories. On every visit to the archives of his memory Cal was amazed at the amount of information available. If I can explain, he felt something like a child must feel who only gets to visit his library when he enters the National Library for the first time.

He liked to visit the memory at night, because when Roberto was asleep many of the neurons were resting and the only ones working were those that were creating dreams.

These had a special, captivating attraction for Cal, perhaps precisely because they are something that atoms do not have.

He was amazed by tricks of the imagination and enjoyed himself like a person sitting in a cinema seat. He liked grandiose dreams; he was ensnared by those beautiful, seductive women; he saw Roberto get lost in mazes which he tried to get out of but couldn't, or climb an endless number of stairs until he came to a very heavy door which he opened with difficulty only to find himself facing a void.

Cal wanted to know more about how the human mind worked and so he exchanged ideas with some of the neurone atoms, who helped him to learn. He discovered that the brain was made up of tens of billions of neurons, as many as there are stars in the Milky Way, and these neurons communicate with each other via a huge number of circuits whose contacts switch on and off two hundred times a second. Two hundred times a second! Unbelievable!

A carbon atom from one of the neurons made the same argument to Calcium that Nitrogen had come up with in those early days:

"The brain is an enormous computer with a capacity that humans have not yet been able to replicate."

For some time, possibly since the period he spent in Francisco's shoulder blade, Cal had not been seized so frequently by doubt. He thought that the carbon atom might be able to help him and so he asked:

"I've been thinking about a human's soul, his individuality. We atoms understand what individuality means as far as we are concerned, but I'm confused in relation to them. What is the soul?"

"It's very simple," replied the anonymous carbon atom. "The soul is nothing but the behaviour of this amazing machine. The joys and sadnesses, memories and ambitions, the sense of identity and freewill, they are all there and nothing more than the expression of this play between sparks and blackouts. Don't try and look for anything else because you won't find it. One day the blood will cease to bring food to these neurons, they will die and the soul will die with them."

The conversation reminded him of the discussions between Francisco and his comrades in the trenches, and his frustration at not being able to communicate with him in that one-way relationship. However, Cal was sure that with Roberto it would be different. First, because now he was not as far away as he had been in the shoulder blade, and second, because he could move freely through the pathways of his mind. And there was another, even more convincing reason: now he was rubbing shoulders with the atoms of his neurons!

He tried one route and then another but he couldn't get through. And the same thing happened for several days. Then he thought that it would be easier to try at night while Roberto was asleep. During one of his dreams he thought for a moment that he had succeeded but Roberto didn't realize and the following morning he had no memory of it. However, the result encouraged him to continue. There were two or three more unsuccessful attempts before finally, one night, he got through.

Roberto was sleeping soundly in the hotel room in Oviedo. He dreamt that he was in his summer holiday home, on the balcony that looks on to the beach. It was night time, the waves were pounding and on the breakers the spray was shining with a phosphorescent light. A pair of binoculars appeared in his hands and he trained them on the light of a boat that was silhouetted against the horizon. It was at that moment that Cal entered the dream. He made himself comfortable, sitting invisibly on the rail of the balcony and said:

"Roberto, I am part of you, I am a calcium atom."

Surprised by the fantasy of the dream, Roberto asked:

"Are you really an atom? What's your name?"

"Those who know me call me Cal"

"How long have you been in my body?"

"No, you misunderstand. I am not *in* your body, I am *part* of you. For a few days I have been part of your blood and I have been going endlessly round and round. I lived in the sea before and I entered your body when you had that tumble on the beach at Aguilar, remember?"

Roberto hesitated for a moment, and said:

"In confidence… can I ask you something? How old are you?"

Cal replied:

"All of the atoms of which you are made are more than a billion years old. I'm one of the younger ones and I'm nearly a billion and fifty, but all your hydrogen atoms are more than thirteen billion. I don't want to upset you, but you should understand that your life is a tiny fraction of eternity, a mere instant in the existence of the Universe. By contrast, the parts of which you are made, your atoms, are almost eternal, or at least that's what we believe… Aren't you a bit jealous of us?"

Roberto hesitated again before replying.

"No, I don't think so. I've always thought that immortality would be unbearable."

"That may be true of immortality; I wouldn't want to be immortal, either. But that's not what I mean. I mean that it would be better to live longer than seventy or eighty. How would you like to live to two hundred, for example? You'd have a fuller, more complete life."

Roberto thought about what it would be like to live for two hundred years knowing at the same time that he was mortal. Immortality seems pointless; knowing that we are mortal makes us enjoy life. Everything we do could be our last act. If we knew we were immortal it would take away our taste for living; everything would be the same, everything would endlessly repeat itself.

"I think you're right, to live for two hundred years wouldn't be at all bad."

In order to console himself in the face of the fleetingness of his existence, Roberto thought about the relatively short life of a bee and other similar nonsense.

Cal thought that it was time to leave the dream. He was about to do so when Elvira kissed Roberto on the cheek and woke him up.

"Get up, it's getting late."

"Elvira, you're not going to believe what I've just been dreaming. I was talking to an atom, it was so real…"

"What a vivid imagination you've got! Why don't I ever have dreams like yours? Well, at least you weren't dreaming about women."

"Why do you say that, Elvira? You know that the only woman I dream about is you…"

That morning the couple planned to leave the hotel in Oviedo to return to Madrid. They would remain there for two or three days and then travel to Miami. It was two days by car with a stop in León. When they got to the Spanish capital night was just falling.

They went into the underground car park of Hotel Wellington in Velázquez Street, arranged their things in their room, rested for a while and decided to go and eat somewhere nearby. They were worn out, especially Roberto. Elvira remembered a very pleasant old-style restaurant, with tables on the sidewalk, in a back street three blocks from the hotel. When they got there Roberto told Elvira again about the dream about the atom. But Cal wasn't paying attention; he was worried by a conversation that he had heard during the car journey. Apparently after the stop in Madrid the journey would continue by plane. This was no small event for him; he would be back in the sky again after a billion years. Despite the time that had elapsed he remembered his journey through space very clearly and the sight of the Earth from high above before he fell into the sea with Oxygen. But since then he had had to content himself with the stories of the atoms that could fly: the hydrogen and oxygen atoms from the water molecules that evaporated from the sea and went around with the clouds, or the atoms from the air's nitrogen molecules. Yes, he was excited; he was going to be in the sky once again…

PART THREE

THE POWER OF FATE

Chaos is order waiting to be deciphered.

JOSE SARAMAGO, *El hombre duplicado*

But Fate's power is mighty and neither wealth nor wars nor castles nor dark ships well-beaten by the waves can escape her.

SOPHOCLES, *Antigone*

In the soul there is no absolute or free will, but the soul is determined to will this or that by a cause which is also determined by another and this again by another and so on to infinity.

SPINOZA, *Ethics*

12

IN THE AIR ONCE AGAIN

The Alberdis spent the last few minutes of their visit to Spain sitting in the uncomfortable seats in the departure lounge of Barajas airport. A few minutes beforehand they had returned the car that they had hired three weeks earlier.

Roberto was reading a crime novel that he had bought the day before in Goya Street. The author, Lawrence Sanders, was his favourite.

The voice on the tannoy announced the departure of the flight to Miami, first in Spanish and then in English. They would spend a week in the United States before returning to Buenos Aires.

Travelling in the same plane was the president of an African country, who was going to take part in a conference on economic development to be held in the Biltmore Hotel in Coral Gables, to the south of Miami. That caused a delay to the boarding, resulting in a protest from the passengers.

As the plane was taxiing along the runway the voice of the chief steward on board went through the usual safety instructions. Roberto, who was a seasoned traveller, only listened to the final words:

"If there is a loss of pressure in the cabin, an oxygen mask will appear in front of you. Place it over your nose and mouth, pull the cord to open the valve and breathe normally."

As always an air stewardess stood at the end of the aisle and accompanied the instructions with graceful movements.

During the take-off and in the first few moments of the flight Roberto gazed out of the window and Cal could look through his eyes. The earth was dropping away as the plane cut through the clouds. What most amused him was to see the molecules of water bumping into the wings, as if this image was bringing his arrival on Earth up to the present.

The spectacle didn't last long; Roberto decided to carry on reading. The book had gripped him from the very first page; however, it took him a long time to concentrate because the passenger in the seat in front of him couldn't keep still. He switched the little individual TV screen on and off, he put the earphones on to listen to some music and then immediately took them off again, he asked for a drink and then before trying it he asked to change it for a different one… Roberto was on the point of asking him for a bit of peace and quiet, but he quickly forgot about it and buried himself in his book once more. The story finally gripped him; while he imagined himself going with Detective McNally along the streets of

Palm Beach, it occurred to him that it would be a good idea to spend a day there while they were in Miami. Elvira loved the mansions by the sea and the stores on Worth Avenue. He figured that if he organized things right they would even have time to have lunch in The Breakers.

When the plane started to descend the voice of the chief steward came over the public address system:

"Ladies and gentlemen, we have started our descent into Miami airport, where we expect to arrive in 30 minutes."

It happened in an instant. The restless passenger jumped up and ran towards the cockpit, knocking over the stewardess who was talking to one of the President's assistants. Sensing danger, Roberto tried to get up from his seat. With his right hand he undid his safety belt and at that precise moment he was blinded by an explosion. The body of the suicide bomber and the front part of the plane's fuselage burst into thousands of pieces. The air was sucked like a tornado through a gaping hole in the roof of the first-class cabin by the almost total vacuum outside. The oxygen masks dropped and were left hanging uselessly. The bodies that were not held down by the safety belt were sucked out and cast into space together with that of the terrorist.

Cal witnessed everything that happened in the plane until Roberto's blood pressure fell to zero. Then his heart tried to carry on beating, but didn't find anything to pump and Cal was pushed out on a gush of blood that dispersed in space, forming a red mist. Millions of ions accompanied him, all of them surrounded by molecules of water protecting them. Cal looked down and saw the blue-green of the sea. Clearly fate was on his side; he was enjoying the luck he had enjoyed so many times before.

Cal thought about the atoms of all the bodies that were falling together with the plane. They were all going to be free again and they would return to the sea to re-join the cycle of Nature. He was right to be happy; if the plane had fallen on the land their fate would have been very different and for many of them it would have been quite awful.

A chloride ion who was falling next to him asked:

"What's going to happen to us?"

"The two of us will be ions of the sea water," Calcium replied. "We'll probably stay there for many centuries, enjoying freedom once more. I'm glad to think that all of the atoms that will fall in the water will enter a new phase – they'll become part of other things: the sea water, the air, a cloud, the sand on the sea bed. Their time spent in the human body will have been one more episode in their existence. They'll soon forget it."

"How long were you in a body?"

"Only for a moment, just about three weeks, but I had the chance to get to know the brain, which is the most interesting part, quite well. I looked in his memory and went through the sixty years of his history."

"And what subjects did you look for in his memory?" asked the chloride ion, rather inquisitively.

"You'll laugh," said Cal. "I tried to find out what he had stored about us atoms… Roberto was an engineer, so he had memorized a lot of information, the names of all the elements, the weights of the most common ones, the way in which we combine to form molecules and hundreds of other pieces of information. But the strange thing is that I didn't find the notion that his body was made of atoms. It appears that it didn't occur to Roberto, and that's why I couldn't find it."

"Incredible," said the chloride ion.

"Although now I come to think of it…" thought Cal, "one night I managed to get into one of his dreams and I told him. Perhaps he will have realized at that moment."

"I think that human beings are not aware that they are put together out of used parts, that none of us atoms was formed in them and that when their life ends, as is happening now, all of us are going to look for somewhere else in Nature to continue with our existence. The strange thing is that all of us atoms were born in different places, we have different histories and ages, and fate brought us together in their body in order to create it. Some of us are there for days, others for months, a few of us for the whole of that person's life. In other words, what lasts in a person is the design, the organization of their structure, but the basic components of that structure - we atoms - are constantly entering and leaving. To put it a better way: when I entered Roberto the atoms of his body and his mind were different from those that he was composed of a few years earlier."

"Talking of that... What were you doing before?

"I was joined to a chlorine atom in a sodium chloride molecule. We lived together for centuries in different places. Before we entered Roberto's body we spent more than a year in a jar of olives. It was nice because we could look at the outside world through the glass. It was the first time that we saw humans. The jar was on a shelf and they used to go past us, until one day Roberto's wife, Elvira, put the jar into a basket. From there we went to their house and you can probably imagine how it ended."

"As well as Roberto I have been part of another human, a young Spaniard. I was also part of a fish, a sea bream... As you can see, I haven't had time to get bored."

"It seems incredible that you've been part of two human beings. Yours must be a unique case among atoms."

"Yes, I am a very unusual case."

Their fall was nearing its end – the surface of the sea seemed to be getting nearer. Cal went on:

"Now, Chloride, we must get ready to fall into the water. I've done it once and I can assure you that it's not much fun. The impact will probably separate us and we won't see each other again. I know that you'll love your new home. I'm looking forward to returning to mine."

13

THE REEF

The return to the sea after an absence of several weeks had taken place in a fairly shallow area near the coast of a small island to the north of the Bahamas. Cal was surprised by the warmth of the water, which was so different from the Cantabrian Sea. It was totally clear and you could see right to the bottom of the sea. It seemed like a garden, but in reality it was a zoo in which the species looked like plants: the sea squirts with their arms like small branches crowned with red globes that look like little fruits; the prickly hydroids; the wrinkled, wavy sponges... However, what really caught Cal's eye was the coral; there were a lot of them and they formed a large reef around the little island.

Amazed by what he saw, Cal was talking about it three days after his arrival in these waters with a calcium ion who knew the area. He told Cal that he and his friends lived in fear of the coral polyps and then he offered to accompany him to the colony to see them at work from close to.

"Stay close to me; they seem harmless, but they're very dangerous," he advised.

There they were, millions of tiny creatures – but huge for Cal – a few millimeters in size, grouped together on the surface of the rocks on the sea-bed. They swept the water with their little tentacles around their small heads. They were looking for food and gobbled it down as soon as they had caught it.

"Why are they dangerous?"

"Because when they swallow food they also swallow water and with it all of the dissolved ions, and we are amongst their favourites. They use us to make calcium carbonate molecules. As these are insoluble in water, they are the ideal material for their underwater constructions."

"I don't understand – what do they construct?"

"It's very simple," said the calcium ion with a knowledgeable air. "They pile up the molecules, with us bound to them, one on top of another, to create platforms and so get higher than their neighbours. The higher they are the more food they get. The calcium atoms are left immobilized in the little columns, so tightly stuck to each other that they seem like a single piece, a skeleton of very strangely shaped stone. Can you see them?"

"It's horrific!" exclaimed Cal.

"Now do you understand why we have to be careful?"

The two of them slowly moved away. The sight of his enslaved fellow atoms made Cal shudder, but there was nothing he could do to help them.

Behind them was the reef. The great underwater edifice of calcium carbonate revealed itself in all its beauty. The shade of red stained on the carbonate seemed to be challenging them.

Over the centuries the coral polyps had piled layer upon layer, always in search of food, unintentionally killing off those below them, the founders of the colony. It was an enormous cemetery, with trillions of calcium atoms condemned to slavery.

Cal spent the following months on the surface of the water, observing the stars by night and talking to his companions. They swam to the bottom – now closer and lit up – to discover new varieties of inhabitants of the sea and amazing themselves every day with the boundless imagination of creation.

It was at that time that Cal celebrated his one billion and fiftieth birthday. I forgot to say that atoms do not celebrate each one of their birthdays, but only every fifty, and their practice is to dedicate that day to meditation. It's a solitary celebration that can either bring about consequences or else go unnoticed. Following their custom, that morning

Cal went back over his history. He was still young and knew that he would exist until the end of the Earth, at least another five billion years. By then the Sun, which was just a small star, would slowly expand: its diameter would grow until it enveloped the nearest planets, probably including the Earth. He would turn into energy and other particles, but it would take a long time. He had a long path ahead of him. However, he felt sad, but he didn't know why.

About midday Cal thought he understood what was happening to him. He had spent the past seventy years living in the fast lane. Perhaps this was the right moment to change his attitude, to concentrate on himself, to spend more time reflecting. Why not stop being an ion and become an atom again? Then he could once again become part of a molecule. Yes, it's true, sometimes you can get tired of being free.

This feeling made him feel strange and odd. He felt a desire to rest, not just for a while but for thousands of years. He would forget the outside world and concentrate on enjoying himself, his own nucleus with its protons and neutrons that he never looked at and within them the quarks and the gluons. Why had he never done so? Why not enjoy in a more conscious way the twenty electrons spinning in their orbits, or get to know his body more closely in a way that he had never felt like doing before? He had made up his mind: he would try to bind his electrons with those of other atoms in order to form a molecule again. Yes, that was his plan for the next few millennia.

But where should he start? He had two or three ideas that he thought about carefully, until he was sure about one of them. It has to be said that it was a crazy idea, but he was used to doing mad things. Much later he would realize how significant this event was for him. But there was nothing that could be done about it; every atom makes mistakes.

He moved slowly, with the water molecules that surrounded him as baggage. He avoided the mouths of the many fish that threatened to swallow him and went close to some enormous shells before slipping on the surface of a sponge. On the reef in the distance the colony of coral polyps were working tirelessly. The tiny creatures, which were smaller than the nail on a little finger, swept the water with their tentacles outstretched in search of food.

Cal approached at the moment when the polyp was swallowing a piece of seaweed and took the opportunity to go in. He never imagined that he could do such a thing so calmly. "It's amazing what the conscience and determination can do," he thought. Once inside he came across oxygen and carbon atoms who immediately embraced him. So, he had achieved his goal; once again he was a complete atom and he was part of a molecule of calcium carbonate.

A few hours later a lot of molecules left the polyp and settled down on millions of identical particles. The process, which was mechanical and immutable, with a few intervals while the polyp rested, left Cal's molecule covered by other carbonates.

So, day by day, very slowly and over tens of years, they formed a small column, one amongst many similar columns, like small-scale skyscrapers in a ghost town. An enormous underwater cemetery: a coral reef.

From then on Cal lost all contact with the outside world. He stopped seeing and once more experienced tranquillity and silence.

The years went by. Even though Cal had learnt to connect with himself better than ever now that he was no longer an ion, his existence in the coral reef left him feeling terribly upset. He was left unable to move, bound as he was into the calcium carbonate molecule together with other atoms. He only felt comfortable with one of them, with Carbon, not only because he was intelligent and amusing, but also because, like him, he knew human beings. The other prisoners were not at all interested; they spent all their time complaining about not being able to move and dreaming about being able to escape one day from their imprisonment in the reef. They were atoms in torment.

Carbon had entered the coral at the same time as Cal in that piece of seaweed swallowed up by the polyp. He knew human beings because for more than fifty years he had been part of the bark of an old tree on the edge of a beach in Florida. From this privileged position, even though it was only for half a century, he had heard them talk, laugh and cry; he had taken pleasure in their embraces and endured their rows. However, his knowledge of human beings was quite superficial, because he had never been part of one. So he found Cal's anecdotes enlightening. What was happening between them was interesting: thanks to Cal's experiences, Carbon was able to complete the knowledge he had acquired just by drawing conclusions from his observations.

According to Carbon a hurricane had pulled the tree up by its roots and hurled it onto the beach. Later the wind and the waves had completed the job so that the piece of bark ended up floating in the sea. After many years and many adventures, which it's not the place to go into here, Carbon became part of the seaweed.

It's important to say that this new friend shared with Cal the misfortune of having been placed, together with the waste from the polyp, in the middle of one of the small columns that made up the reef. Because they were in the middle surrounded by thousands of identical carbonates and a long way from the surface that was in contact with the water, neither of them had any connection with the molecules or the ions of the dissolved salts, which could have given them news of what was happening on the outside, just like in earlier times. Unfortunately for the two friends the atoms around them, their only direct link, were perfect ignoramuses. News reached them via an endless chain. The atom that was on the coral's surface chatted with those travelling the seas and afterwards sent the message that started to go around the column from the outside towards the centre, from one atom to the next and so on like in a relay race. When the news reached them, having covered the distance of a millimeter, it had been passed on via thousands of atoms. On the way every intermediary added something of his own and the next one forgot some important detail. As you can imagine the message that they finally received had very little to do with the original version. To cap it all, as none of the atoms in the chain had been part of a human being, when the news included a reference to humans the atoms didn't understand what it was about and were incapable of conveying exactly what they heard.

So the news was confined to the temperature of the sea water, the rate of growth of the reef, an enormous fish that had attacked and bitten the coral cemetery, the attempt to escape captivity by an atom prisoner who was on the surface of the column and who had failed - and other topics like these.

One day Cal thought that some of his electrons were going to break away from him. The last atom in the chain of communication with the outside world said very agitatedly:

"Hey, Cal! There's a warning that a very rare fish that has never been seen before is charging into the reef... but it's not biting it, it's hitting it with one of its fins! It has a round head and every so often it blows bubbles of air from its mouth!"

The last atom went on:

"Now they're saying that it was able to break off a piece, that it took it with its two front fins and then it disappeared"

Cal looked at Carbon in astonishment.

"Don't get upset, Cal," said Carbon, "it won't do you any good. Let them enjoy their ignorance, unless you feel able to make them understand what the underwater swimming means?"

From then on, they wearily decided to take no notice of the outside world. And although they felt relaxed about their attitude, it also increased their isolation. They had turned in upon themselves, deaf to the whispering of their atom neighbours.

14

ATOMIC THOUGHTS

The two atoms were so wrapped up in their own thoughts that they spent years without talking to each other. Until one day and without warning Carbon broke the silence.

"Hey, Cal!"

"What?"

"Recently, that is over this past year, I was thinking that I'd like to discuss the subject of fate with you again."

Like any reasonably informed atoms they both knew the laws that governed their existence. Fate was one of their favourite subjects. They knew that the Universe had been formed thirteen thousand seven hundred million years earlier in an initial act that human beings, curiously, called the Big Bang. The two atoms didn't like this expression because they found it confusing; it seemed to indicate that the Cosmos had started to exist following an explosion in an extremely dense part of space, and they asked themselves: how could a point in space exist at that time if space didn't yet exist?

However, there was something that they were sure of: from its very beginning the Universe had begun a process of expansion that continued into the present. The galaxies were moving away from each other at incredible speeds and would continue to do so in the future, for hundreds of billions of years, until all the stars had gone and turned the Cosmos into an almost infinite expanse, with all of its matter, cold and without light, wandering around in space.

The origin of the Universe had always been a great mystery for the atoms from their earliest days. When Cal used to receive his first lessons from Hydrogen, it occurred to him one day to ask him to explain.

"The origin of the Universe?" his teacher had replied with surprise. "I don't know; no-one knows. We shall never know. It's an unfathomable enigma that will last forever. If you ever hear anyone say that they know, don't believe them, because they will be lying to you."

In their discussion about fate, Cal and Carbon were optimistic and were convinced that the work of creation was never-ending and was not confined to the formation of the Universe in which they lived. They asked themselves this type of question: Why should ours be the only universe? They shared the view that at any moment a new universe was being born and that the number of universes that coexisted was infinite, although they couldn't prove it. They believed that there had always been universes, including before the Big Bang, and that there always would be, ad infinitum.

However, they didn't manage to agree on one fundamental question: were all the universes different from each other, or were they, on the other hand, the same as theirs? On this point, Carbon believed that if creation used the same basic elements and imposed on them the same laws, the resulting universes would have to be copies of the previous ones. He was excited by the idea that everything that he knew had already existed and would exist again and that they would exist an infinite number of times. The truth is that there was nothing wrong with thinking like that. He always said to Cal:

"You'll be back in Francisco's shoulder-blade time and again, and every time a bullet will rip you out of his body and throw you in the sea."

Cal enjoyed contradicting him. He said he didn't believe in the repetition of identical universes, although he shared the belief about the infinite number of distinct universes. His argument was very simple:

"Creation can't be so boring as to always repeat the same piece of work. Suppose that in other universes the force that keeps the proton and neutrons of our nuclei together had a different value, or that the total mass that makes up each universe was different, or that heaven knows what other variable that we take as a constant were changed. Any universe that resulted from such a creation would be nothing like the one that we know."

Oxygen, one of the atoms that formed part of the calcium carbonate molecule (together with Carbon, Cal and two other oxygen atoms) stood out because of his excessive shyness. He had never communicated with them. He was much older, since he had been born somewhere in the Milky Way more than four and a half billion years ago, whereas (let's remember) Cal was little more than a billion. In addition he had travelled through space for centuries together with another atom like him, together forming an oxygen molecule until they reached the Earth, when the planet was in the process of being formed. This oxygen molecule had encountered an atmosphere that was totally different from the present one: at that time there was a lot of water vapour, methane, ammonia, nitrogen and other gases, but there were only traces of oxygen. Oxygen and his friend mixed with those gases and remained there for millions of years watching the planet complete its formation (Cal and Carbon found out about all this after their discussion, because up to that time Oxygen still remained silent). By means of a long process the composition of the atmosphere changed; some gases almost disappeared, the water vapour condensed as a liquid and fell on the surface, and the percentage of oxygen increased considerably. This change meant that Oxygen and his companion had the opportunity to head towards the surface of the sea more often. One day when they were enjoying themselves brushing against the crest of a wave they ventured further than they should and the water molecules caught them. More or less at this time Cal arrived on the Earth. The two oxygen atoms had a major fright when the water molecules surrounded them. They didn't understand what had happened. But it was very simple: the molecule of gas had dissolved in the water.

They were never able to escape and return to the atmosphere; they were stuck with their existence in the sea. Since then, the two of them together and without the freedom enjoyed by the ions had been mere spectators of the events lived through by Cal.

When they passed through the mouth of the coral polyp and bumped into the piece of seaweed that the creature was swallowing, Oxygen noticed that next to him a calcium ion was looking at him with indifference. Of course he didn't know that the metabolism of that tiny creature would end up by binding them together in the same calcium carbonate molecule. Once inside the polyp Oxygen felt that other atoms were attacking them. His regular friend disappeared from his side; someone had pulled him from the molecule to bind him into another one. He never found out what happened to him - whether he remained imprisoned in the reef or if he was able to return to the sea. But in a way he felt liberated; he had always depended on the other oxygen atom, who was stronger and more impulsive. Perhaps this had been the cause of his excessive timidity.

On the day of the discussion about fate, when Cal explained to Carbon his view about the universes being distinct from ours, they were interrupted by Oxygen's harsh voice.

"Cal, may I ask you a question?"

Cal and Carbon looked at him in shock, without uttering a word. It was the first time in almost a hundred years of being bound to them that Oxygen had opened his mouth. Oxygen was clearly anxious because he went on:

"If it's no bother, could you explain about this question of fate?"

"What do you want to know for?" Cal replied aggressively.

"The thing is, I've seen you so engaged with the subject that I'd like to be able to join in the conversation. I know I haven't got your intelligence or experience, and I must confess I'm a bit jealous. But if we're going to be here for billions of years - and so far we've only been here for about a hundred – I think that if I don't change I'm not going to be able to stand it. I have to decide to talk and know more in order to be able to understand my identity. So please help me to do that.

Carbon, whose fifty years in the bark of a tree had endowed him with the virtues of tolerance and compassion, didn't hesitate to respond on behalf of them both.

"Of course, Oxygen, Cal will help you."

Cal understood his friend's gesture and wondered about Oxygen's position. He was also sorry to see him so fearful about the future.

"Before I tell you what all of us atoms have learned about fate – and I see that you have forgotten – I want to reassure you. When I arrived in the coral more than ninety years ago, I thought that I would be staying here for a few millennia. A very turbulent period of my life was coming to an end and I needed time and a place to rest. But for some months I have had the feeling that something different is going to happen and that in a short time – in about a century or two – everything is going to change for us for the better. Besides, the Earth is going to exist for another five billion years, maybe more, until the Sun dies, so it is very likely that we will survive until then. You're going to have plenty of time to find out about everything."

After that Oxygen looked at him with relief. Cal went on talking quite naturally:

"I'll explain it to you in very simple terms so that you can understand. The reality is rather more complex and in time you'll be able to find out all about it. I'll start with our ideas about creation. Let's see. The three of us and all the other types of atoms, except for the hydrogens, the heliums and a few lithiums, were born in the body of stars that were about to die. Our nuclei were formed by the fusion of helium nuclei. Our different atomic types resulted from the number of nuclei that fused to create us. But the Universe was formed a long time before we were born."

"I don't understand," said Oxygen. "Can you go more slowly?"

"Yes, of course. Where did you lose track?"

"About the formation of the Universe..."

"Well, I was going to say that in this initial act - about whose origins there's only guesswork - matter and energy, space and time were born."

"When? What happened?"

"It was almost fourteen billion years ago. In a fraction of a second space seemed to inflate like a balloon and its temperature suddenly fell. This drop in temperature meant that elementary particles of matter – quarks - were able to join together to form neutrons and protons. A short time later they combined, producing the simplest atomic nuclei."

"And the temperature continued to fall?"

"Precisely. And when it reached a critical point, tens of thousands of years later, the nuclei (with a positive electric charge) were surrounded by electrons (with a negative electric charge) to form our ancestors: hydrogen atoms, those of his brother deuterium, and helium and lithium atoms."

"Now I understand why you said before that those atomic species were the exception."

"Of course, because they were born practically at the same time as the Universe and are much older than ours. But they are still living with us and have been and are our teachers."

Oxygen said nothing. Cal went on:

"Now I'll tell you our ideas about fate. If we argue that all of the initial particles were given clearly defined properties and that the relationship between them was also defined by immutable physical laws, we have to accept that their future and the future of the whole group was predetermined. This particular feature is what we call fate. The result is everything that you see, for example, the three of us, the coral prison of which we are a part, the sea, the creatures that live in it, as well as ideas, the conversation, feelings, the movement of the waves."

Oxygen was about to say something when Cal added:

"But I have to be honest with you – we don't all think the same. There are some atoms with a mind of their own who have their own ideas that are different from those of the majority. A typical example of them is Phosphorus, a good friend of mine whom I haven't seen for some considerable time. Phosphorus and I met in the stomach of a fish and we stayed joined together in a molecule of calcium phosphate. We were part of a human bone, the shoulder blade of Francisco, a young man with whom we shared countless adventures. Phosphorus was very introverted; he could go for weeks without saying a word, although not for as long as you. Much later I realized that he devoted all that time to meditation. Phosphorus believed in the existence of a Creator of the Universe and defined him in this way:

'All of us atoms, and consequently the Universe, were created by something superior to ourselves, by a Being that has no need of any other reason to exist, who is infinite and has infinite faculties, as well as being perfect. His work is limited to creating the basic elements of matter, such as electrons and quarks, and to establish in them the laws that determine their behaviour. He also created space so that they could exist and time so that their existence could take place. After this initial act the Creator only manifests himself through the outcome of that creation, which is nothing other than the continuous evolution of reality.' "

"That means," Oxygen interrupted, "that the Creator that your friend Phosphorus believes in decides what's happening and what's going to happen and determines the course of our fate."

"No, wait, it's not like that. This so-called Creator can only consider the outcome, which becomes evident in the course of time with the unfolding of events. Put another way, at some point we are going to leave this reef at a time and due to some circumstance that are predetermined. But that time and the way in which we will leave cannot be changed, nor can they be predicted. They will be the consequence of an almost infinite number of causal links by an almost infinite number of actors and actions. The Creator is not going to change them because he cannot; in order to do so he would have to change something already created, which would be a contradiction. Don't forget that he and consequently his work – according to Phosphorus' view – are perfect."

"Let me think about that for a while," begged Oxygen, who was somewhat confused and rather worn out.

But Cal went on enthusiastically:

"I'll help you with another example... I know! I'll tell you what human beings think about fate, because it's similar to what you just meant with your question... You're not a human in disguise, are you?" he joked.

"No, no way," said Oxygen, "it's pure coincidence."

"I'm glad to hear it," said Cal with the superior air of a teacher. "Well, I'll tell you. Some human beings don't believe in anything, they drift through their existence without feeling their lives to be predetermined. Others assume that fate is uncertain and undefined. Others are determinists, almost fatalists. But the vast majority of humans, those who matter for the purposes of what I am trying to explain, are convinced that their fate depends on the will of God, an all-powerful and omnipresent being who created them. Humans attribute to their God the power of will and desire, the capacity to love and hate, to reward and punish. They believe that God decides the fate of each one of them as they live their life. They imagine him to be like them (they even give him human form!) and believe that they can ask favours, from resolving the most trivial thing to the most significant. They are convinced that he listens to them and then, like a judge, he either grants it to them or refuses them. They imagine him seated in the vastness of the heavens and suddenly looking down to see a pale blue dot lost in the immensity of the

Universe, on the edge of one of the almost infinite number of galaxies that he had created, and from that tiny planet he chooses one of the billions of tiny creatures that live there – it could be a human being or an insect – and then he can decide that it is time for that person or that butterfly to cease to exist."

"It's rather absurd," said Oxygen, "but you can't deny that they have a powerful imagination."

"The thing is that human beings are rather arrogant and think that they were created by a god, when what is certain is that it is humans who created their gods. The strange thing for me is that they haven't realized that they appeared thirteen billion years after the Creation and that they represent a barely perceptible detail in the Universe."

Carbon, who had followed the account without interrupting it, decided that this was the moment to intervene:

"Oxygen, I have to tell you that Cal and I have discussed the subject of humans and religion many times and we have not been able to agree. As you will have seen Cal rather sneers at religious people, but I think he's wrong. He applies rationalist criteria in order to judge them, but he applies it badly; he does not realize that religious belief in human beings occurs on a level that is completely different from the beliefs of everyday life. That's why I believe that religious arguments do not make sense; they are a waste of time, and faith in a human being does not brook any discussion.

Cal said nothing and the conversation began to flag, while Oxygen tried to absorb all of the ideas and felt grateful to his companions. Why had he waited almost a hundred years to ask them to help him to think?

At that moment a piece of news reached them via the chain of atoms: a very powerful storm was blowing in the waters of the Caribbean.

"Maybe it's a hurricane," said Carbon. "After all, it is September. When the wind uprooted my tree it was September…

Oxygen could not help revealing his innocence and said:

"Will this hurricane be sufficiently strong to pull up the reef from the bottom of the sea and free us from this imprisonment?"

15

THE ESCAPE

It was midday on 4 December 2305. They had been stuck in their coral prison for more than three hundred years. Nothing had changed.

At twelve o'clock precisely a powerful earthquake shook the reef and seconds – or perhaps it was a full minute – later, it started to collapse. The small column of calcium carbonate that had accommodated them, together with many other similar columns, broke into thousands of pieces.

After almost three centuries Cal and his two friends saw the outside world once again. The sea-water molecules flowed alongside them and some ions made fun of the rigidity imposed upon them by that small fragment of coral which, suspended in the water, moved aimlessly in the midst of great confusion.

The din was unbearable. After so many years of silence the noise enveloped them in a distressing way. They could understand very little about what was happening. Then Cal noticed something strange: the water of the Caribbean, which he remembered as being so clear that the Sun lit up the bottom of the sea, had completely clouded over. The cause was an enormous machine that was destroying part of the reef.

Behind the windows of the cabin Cal made out the face of a human. It reminded him of being surrounded by mist that summer's morning in Asturias, when through it he saw a tractor moving rocks to block the road. He didn't have time to think because the machine's enormous shovel hoisted him out of the sea together with his friends. In the air the sky seemed bluer than ever.

The planned construction was huge: an underwater hotel in the middle of the reef, with see-through walls so that the visitors were in contact with the sea bed and could enjoy – and almost touch - the coral and the multi-coloured fishes. In the first phase of the work the part of the reef where the hotel would be built was being destroyed by bulldozers that were working under the sea; their mechanical shovels, like enormous sieves, were straining the material and loading it on to transporters that were piling it on to the beach of the little island.

The whole surface of the island would be turned into the huge reception area of the underwater hotel, with an airport for vertical take-off and landing aircraft. Tourists would come from all over the world. The calcium carbonate extracted from the reef would be used to reinforce the surface of the runway. Cal and his friends faced a tragic future; they were leaving the cemetery made of coral only to be dumped in another one.

They were fortunate, for on the surface of the little island they remained on top. They continued looking at the sky without saying a word. A water molecule that was floating in the humid air came up to them, and when one of its hydrogen atoms saw that Oxygen was trapped and helpless, he couldn't help showing some compassion.

"I'll tell you what's going to happen," said the unknown atom to Oxygen. "It's serious but don't be scared."

Oxygen broke his silence:

"Please…"

"In less than about an hour they're going to take you to the entrance of that enormous tower, the one you can see on your right. It's a machine used for crushing and drying the material extracted from the coral. First of all you'll be ground to dust and then you'll feel a current of warm air. I know that tower very well because I went round it several times. The current of air will draw off all of the water molecules towards the atmosphere and you will fall on to that other pile of dry material, the one you can see behind the tower. If you land there you'll be lost, because at the next stage you'll be mixed with other materials and laid down as tarmac on the surface of the runway. Then other layers of material will come down on top of you and you'll be buried there for ever and ever."

Cal and Carbon looked at each other in an atomic way. Oxygen listened to the explanation very attentively. The hydrogen atom went on:

"The only way to escape is to slip out through the chimney of the dryer. It's difficult, but you have to try. I know that a few have managed to do it."

Cal and Carbon, who were worried about how close things were to coming to an end and astonished at how unemotional Oxygen was, thought that the calm that Oxygen was displaying was due to his experience of spending billions of years in the atmosphere, and specifically to his knowledge that he was an atom that was capable of flying.

Cal entrusted his fate to Oxygen's experience. Who would have said that two hundred years earlier!

"What do you think we should do?"

"I am looking at the column of air coming out of the drying tower. If you look carefully," said Oxygen, "you'll see the molecules of the oxygen atoms, the nitrogen atoms of the air and many molecules of the water evaporated from the coral. Also, hidden amongst them, you'll see other particles that are much bigger than the molecules."

There was a brief silence. Oxygen went on:

"Look at the sparkle from that one," he said suddenly. "If I'm not mistaken, it's from a microscopic piece of calcium carbonate. However perfect the system may be to trap the particles in the air outlet of the dryer, some of them – a very few – manage to escape!"

Cal and Carbon looked at him in amazement. How badly they had judged good old Oxygen with his superior attitude in the early years on the reef. Oxygen had something that they didn't have, or at least, not on this occasion: an admirable capacity for observation and analysis. What use now were all their explanations about God and fate? No use at all; it was time to act! At the time when Oxygen had asked Cal to explain the history of creation, Cal had shared everything he knew with his friend. Now the situation gave Oxygen the chance to do something in return: the possibility of helping them by offering them something of his experience and his courage.

They decided on a plan of action. They were in a minute fragment of coral and they knew that the smaller it was the better their chances of escape. Oxygen explained the strategy to them. When they went into the grinding machine they had to convince the atoms that formed their particle to head for one of the blades and allow it to strike them mercilessly so that it would crush the piece of coral until it was reduced to a fine powder.

And that is what happened. They received hundreds of terrible blows from the blades that spun round at a great speed. When the crushing had finished there were scarcely a few thousand atoms left in the particle - now invisible to the human eye - where the three friends had been. After their beating, just as the unidentified hydrogen atom had said, a very warm current of air dragged them off and they remained suspended in an enormous chamber. They went up and down doing somersaults in space. The water molecules started to evaporate and then abandoned them, forming part of the humid air that was going out of the chimney. When the particle lost the weight of the water that provided its moisture, the current of air started to lift it up. The decisive moment was approaching; soon they would know what fate had in store for them…

Oxygen warned them:

"We're about to enter the separator which comes before the exit chimney. The centrifugal force will try to push us against the walls. The nearer we are to the centre the more chance we'll have of escaping. Let's make one final effort!"

He knew that they could not do anything; he was just trying to encourage them. The die was cast and their fate depended on the trajectory and the size of the particle in which they were trapped.

Suddenly they found themselves enveloped in the midst of a violent whirlwind. The largest particles were thrown against the sides of the separator, bounced off and fell into the abyss. The smallest were subjected to a tussle between forces: the centrifugal force that held them back and the upward force that set them free. In the background a circle of deep blue outlined at the top of the chimney showed them the escape route.

Gradually the blue circle started to get bigger until finally it was no longer a circle and became the whole sky. The current of warm air had carried them out of the dryer. It is no exaggeration to say that Oxygen's experience and courage had saved them from disaster.

The particle that they were in was so small that it floated in the air like an aerosol. It was made up of a few thousand molecules of calcium carbonate that had managed to join in the escape.

From up on high they looked down on the small island. The machines were spreading the material on the ground and then the rollers were flattening it to form the airport runway. It was a terrifying sight.

PART FOUR

THE FUTURE

Whether or not I survive, I know my atoms are likely to return to the ocean depths. What happens to them after I cease to exist is beyond my control, and their future seems inexorably written, regardless of my own hopes and dreams. I am only a temporary abode and my life is an inconsequential moment in their vast eternity.

LAWRENCE M. KRAUSS, *Atom*

By the year 2099 there will no longer be any clear distinction between humans and computers. Most conscious entities will not have a permanent physical presence. Machine-based intelligences derived from extended models of human intelligence will claim to be human.

RAY KURZWEIL, *The Age of Spiritual Machines*

Give me a place to stand and I will move the Earth.

ARCHIMEDES

16

IN THE YEAR 2305

It was four o'clock in the afternoon when the sky began to cloud over. The east wind was carrying the clouds towards the land. After travelling alone for a couple of hours, the particle finally found itself caught up with the water molecules of a very thin, almost transparent cloud.

While Oxygen was beginning to understand the meaning of fate, Carbon felt happy to have regained his freedom and Cal, feeling nervous, was unable to forget the face of the man in the cab of the underwater tractor. He looked around him and wondered what had happened on Earth during the last three centuries - and with good reason.

An old hydrogen atom, who was talking to his friends from a water molecule, said to him with some sympathy:

"What's up? Don't tell me, I can imagine... it must be very sad to find yourself stuck among so many atoms in a ridiculous particle. But look on the bright side: in spite of your misfortune you can float in the air; you're not shut in."

Cal took some comfort from his words and asked him:

"Where are you from? What has happened to you in the last three hundred years?"

"I imagine that you know all about hydrogen atoms. We're all old and a bit scatter-brained, but I think I'm a special case: I'm a faithful atom. I've lived with this hydrogen atom that you see next to me and with this oxygen atom as a water molecule since the Earth was formed. That's more than five billion years.... And you know something? As fate would have it we never stayed still, we never ended up on dry land, we were never on the ground, in an aquifer, a plant, an animal, or of course, a human being."

Cal looked at him in surprise. The unknown hydrogen atom went on:

"We've floated in the air, either as humidity or as a cloud, and then the rain has returned us to the sea. We spent the last two centuries in the sea until one fine day we decided we would evaporate – as you know, that's quite a common decision for a water molecule. We moved close to the surface, waited until the Sun heated us up and then took off. So once again we got to a cloud. That's happened to us millions of times..." - the hydrogen atom paused; he liked to show off. "Why ask me about the last three hundred years? They weren't the most important."

The old atom's spontaneity and sincerity encouraged Cal to open up:

"The particle that we're in is a piece of a coral reef. My friends and I were trapped in it for three hundred years, totally cut off from everything. That's why I'm asking you what's happened in the past few centuries, because I have no idea. Thanks to fate, as you say, this morning some humans destroyed the reef and by chance saved us. I can tell you that I know human beings well; I formed part of two of them. I think I must be a unique case among atoms, unless you know one that's been in two humans."

"No, not in two, but I do have friends who have been part of one of them. I was with the last one – a sodium ion that I met in the Mediterranean – just recently. We separated again when my two companions decided to take off again. I've been travelling since then."

When Hydrogen had finished talking, a beach appeared in the distance towards the West. The waves were breaking and then disappearing on the sand. They were reaching land. The Sun was going down on the horizon and darkness was spreading as night fell. The cloud was now much thicker and more compact and the water molecules bumped into one another. First one knocked into the molecule containing his new Hydrogen friend, followed by other strong but friendly blows which moved it away from Cal. Hydrogen tried to wave goodbye and managed to shout:

"It's just about to start to rain! Soon we'll become part of a drop of water; warn your friends to get ready for the fall! At the speed we're going and given how near we are to the coast I think that we're about to make history: for the first time in five billion years we're going to fall on dry land!"

An electric discharge made Cal, Carbon and Oxygen shudder. The drops of water were getting bigger and one of them dragged them into the descent, while the wind took them away from the coast. A real storm was lashing Florida, and the drop with the particle carrying the three friends was in the middle of a whirlwind.

The only one with any experience of similar circumstances was Oxygen, who had been in millions of storms when he was younger.

"Keep calm, nothing can happen to us," he said to encourage them. "We've got to prepare ourselves for the blow when we hit the ground and then we'll see what to do."

But there was no blow and they hardly felt any impact. The drop of water - and with it the piece of calcium carbonate - had fallen on the water on the surface of a lake. The three of them had the same thought: 'calcium carbonate is insoluble in water, we can't get out of this prison, we shall slowly slide down to the bottom and remain trapped again, perhaps forever'.

Kissimmee is a small lake in the centre of the Florida peninsula, surrounded by other small lakes. The evening storm made the water choppy when the rain began to fall. The speed of the falling particle caused it to go. down two or three meters below the surface of the lake However, it didn't carry on falling to the bottom; it remained suspended together with millions of other tinier particles that clouded the water that had been stirred up by the storm.

As if they had come to an agreement, Cal, Carbon and Oxygen waited together for the next twist of fate to reveal itself...

It didn't take long. The attack was unexpected; it felt as if tiny creatures were pecking at the piece of calcium carbonate they were in. Their molecule was on the surface of the particle, so they were the first to feel the strong, persistent stabs. It wasn't fish or molluscs, but atoms just like them: carbons, oxygens and also thousands of atoms of hydrogen.

They heard one of them saying:

"We've come to liberate you – don't be afraid."

In the water there were millions of molecules of dissolved carbon dioxide. They had arrived from the atmosphere mixed with the air which was propelled by the machinery designed to combat pollution in the lake. As it comes into contact with the water, the carbon dioxide from the air is transformed into carbonic acid, and it was specifically its ions that were attacking them. It was an unequal struggle and after a few minutes thousands of calcium carbonate molecules from the particle had been chopped into pieces. The result was that Cal and all of the atoms like him had once more been transformed into ions. After three centuries, Cal had become a calcium ion again.

Carbon and Oxygen, together with the two oxygen atoms that had always accompanied them in the molecule, plus one of the attackers – a hydrogen atom – formed a large, heavy ion but one which, in spite of that, was able to move freely: a bicarbonate ion. Although the two friends were handcuffed, they had managed to escape from their prison. They were like those fugitives who have managed to break out of jail but are still in irons and a heavy chain.

Cal, who was once again surrounded by water molecules that were protecting him and who was much more agile than his companions' bicarbonate ion, had fun going round and round them. They swapped harmless jibes:

"Oxygen, you must be careful with Carbon's stories; don't let yourself be taken in by his idea of several universes, it's a complete lie."

"You'll get bored with your freedom, Cal," replied Oxygen. "When you're tired of going round in circles you'll come and talk to us again."

"I've got a better idea," said Cal. "Remember what I told you about my games with the foam on the crest of the waves? Well, I reckon that it must be much more fun if one of those giant aeration machines sucks you in with its pump and blows you out through the air in one of its water jets. Now I'm going to go for a spin near the coast; I want to find out where we've landed and what's happening around us."

During the course of several months, Cal went round and round. He went close to the shore, he played with the jets of water from the aeration machines and he talked with a lot of ions. The ions explained to him where in the world he had fallen, why the water was cloudy, what varieties of fish were to be found in the lake and other interesting information. However, he heard nothing of significance about human beings, only generalities. During all that time he didn't meet a single atom that had been part of one.

Gradually he stopped meeting Carbon and Oxygen. In the last three hundred years they had told each other everything there was to tell and they had discussed every subject under the sun. He was thinking about this when a strange and totally silent type of motorboat passed close by. As he watched it move away and tried to work out how it was powered, he heard a strange voice next to him.

"Hello," said the newcomer.

"Hello," Cal replied, surprised by his rapid adjustment, and asked him: "Who are you?" "Where are you from?"

"I am a sodium ion and have just left the body of a human being. We were travelling in the motor boat that's just gone by."

"I was also part of one!" exclaimed Cal excitedly. "How did you enter him?"

"I used to be part of a sodium chloride molecule. With Chloride we spent almost all of our life in a salt mine. We were resigned to spending the rest of our days there when someone rescued us. I shan't tell you the whole story because it's very long, but the thing is that we found ourselves in a salt cellar and from there we ended up in John's body."

"Mine happened more than three hundred years ago. Tell me, have humans changed much in the last few hundred years?"

"How can I know if they've changed if the first time I've entered one of them was only just six months ago?" said Sodium with a logic that Cal found irrefutable. "I don't know what they were like in the past…"

This hadn't occurred to Cal. Then he thought that if Sodium told him things about the recent life of this person, he would be able to compare them with his experiences in Roberto and Francisco. In that way he would have a rough idea of what had happened. Three hundred years was a long time for humans, he thought, representing more than ten generations!

"Tell me about John. How old is he?"

"John Davis is his full name and he's eighty-four."

"He's an old man."

"Don't you believe it. In six years' time he'll stop working as he's thinking of retiring. As you know," said Sodium, without anticipating that Cal's figures could be very different, "humans live to between a hundred and fifteen and a hundred and twenty years old, and they stop work at ninety. They work quite a lot – between three and four hours a day."

"What does John do?" was a key question. Without realizing it Cal was turning into a good detective.

"His company specializes in underwater projects. At the moment John is managing the construction of a hotel in the Bahamas."

In the atomic world, incidentally, coincidences happen about once in a thousand years.

"Does he travel very often?" was the next question from Cal, who was more anxious to know about humans than to talk about his personal adventures.

"Travel? No, he never travels," said Sodium. "He does everything from the same place, via the screens that cover the walls of his office. That's where he receives instructions, discusses plans, gives orders. The others appear before him. They seem natural but they are virtual images. The funniest one is fat and bald, Engineer Brines, who lives on the island where they're building the hotel."

"Is the one who takes the decisions older than John?"

"Who, the manager of the company? No, he has no age. He's not human, he's an artificial intelligence - an AI, as they say. His name is George. He has a very pleasant, deep voice. When he wants to be more precise, his written instructions appear on one of the screens."

Cal felt confused. It was clear that things had changed a lot in the last three hundred years.

"Can you explain what an AI is? Who's George?"

"To be honest I don't know who he is. They say that he's a system and I have to accept that. What I can tell you is that George is highly intelligent and has a prodigious memory and can make a decision in a flash."

"Where does George live?"

"As I understand it he doesn't live anywhere. He is the expression of several intelligences that are interconnected in order to bring together their memories and their powers of reasoning. Were there computers three hundred years ago?"

"Yes, Roberto was always talking about them."

"Well, I've heard that more than a hundred years ago the intelligence of a computer was greater than the intelligence of humans. The simplest explanation I can give you about George is that he represents the synthesis of several of these computers working together. What's more, from then on these strange new entities had ideas that humans had never had before. They could solve problems that humans were not capable of solving and gradually their importance in human society grew."

"But... who wields the power?"

"That's a good question. Although the human brain hasn't changed much in recent times, a group of individuals were able to increase their capacity for observation and memory with neural implants. John Davis is one of them. This group retains power and for the time being controls intelligent beings who, as I said, are not organic. Now that you mention it, John is always discussing the subject of power with fatty Brines..."

"And what do they say?"

"John says that human beings will always exercise control over decision-making and that they will go on integrating with the Artificial Intelligences to create a new species that will outdo the present one. These individuals of the future will retain their personality, with the ability of humans to feel and to love, but their intelligence, which will be increasingly less biological, will become unbelievably powerful... According to John these new beings will continue the task started by humans in the development of intelligence on the planet. But Brines doesn't agree: he says that that way of thinking is utopian, that it won't be long before the Artificial Intelligences decide to take their own decisions and that when it happens the fate of humans will be in danger. Brines believes the human race will soon depend completely on the artificial beings and consequently they will have no option but to accept their decisions. From then on the unthinkable could happen. He's a pessimist; he sees no reason to assume that these new beings will be compassionate and kind with beings that are so inferior to them."

"What else does Brines say?"

"That the Artificial Intelligences will continue to evolve while human beings do not. And in a few hundred years time they will be mobile and not static as they are now. He also says that when they are able to reproduce by themselves they will be all powerful."

At that moment Cal thought of another matter that had once fascinated him and said:

"When I was part of Francisco, together with my friends, we were intrigued by human sexuality, something that we atoms don't have. I remember Francisco's meetings with Beatriz, a very young woman that he was crazy about. What's John like in that respect? Is he married?"

It was the first time that Sodium had heard the word 'married' and although he didn't understand what it meant, he did understand the sense of the question.

"John enjoys sex, of course. His partner is Jacqueline, a delightful woman."

"Do they live together?"

"No, John lives alone, like all humans that I've come across. To be precise, he doesn't exactly live alone. His assistant, an almost human robot, also lives in his house."

"Tell me about Jacqueline."

"She lives a long way away in a city called Quebec. They share nearly every night with each other. John has one of the latest virtual reality models set up in his house and he has set up the same thing in Jacqueline's apartment. They choose where they are going to meet each time. The place they like most is a beach in the Caribbean. They make love and then go to sleep."

"What language do they use?"

Sodium looked at him uncomprehendingly:

"Each of them speaks their own language and the other listens in their own. Wasn't it like that before?"

Cal was astounded.

"You said that humans live for almost one hundred and twenty years, forty years longer than when I knew them."

"Perhaps that has to do with the fact that they perfected the use of nanorobots?"

"Nanorobots?" Cal's tone made it clear to Sodium that he didn't know what they were.

"They are tiny creatures, constructed atom by atom and molecule by molecule. Once they've been made, they receive instructions on how to work which are recorded in their memory. Then, to make them work, they are injected into the blood stream to help the humans' immune system. They are specialized: some destroy pathogenic microbes, others attack carcinogenic cells and yet others arterial plaques…"

"Of course, now I understand why humans live longer…."

"They are injected millions at a time," said Sodium.

"How do they produce millions?"

"They make a few nanorobots that act as a model, fine-tune them, test them, and once they are satisfied that everything is functioning as planned, they instruct them to reproduce themselves. It's all very simple. In a few days there are millions of them."

"And what are human beings concerned about? Something must worry them…"

"I know that humans are afraid that they will lose control of the process and they won't be able to stop it. I have listened to numerous conversations on the subject and, according to what I've heard, it would seem that the risks are very high. It is likely that one day, because of some error in the program of the nanorobots' intelligence, they will turn into a plague that will destroy other creatures."

Listening to Sodium, the first conclusion that Cal came to was that humans were the only thing on Earth that had undergone change. The sky was the same, and so were the Moon, the Sun, the tides, the stars, the clouds and the storms; even the temperature was just as he remembered it. It was neither hotter nor colder than three hundred years earlier.

But Cal was mistaken. In what was a very short time in the life of an atom, humans had colonized the Moon and Mars, they had developed new means of transport and set up space stations that were proper cities with thousands of inhabitants. Huge reflectors positioned in space focused solar energy on to electrical generators mounted on the planet's surface. In addition they had succeeded in controlling environmental pollution and notable advances had been made in biology, as well as new techniques in human reproduction. When Cal found out about all of that he would certainly find it hard to believe.

After a pause Sodium suggested they go and play with the water pumps from the aeration machines. On the way they noticed that the water was moving in another direction, as if a much more powerful pump was attracting them. Their curiosity proved to be disastrous.

"This machine must be amazing," exclaimed Cal.

But it turned out not to be the aspirator of an aeration machine but the water suction pipe of a pump set up on the bank of the lake. Cal and Sodium found that they were starting to move at great speed, and a few moments later they felt the regular force of the metal blades of the centrifugal pump. The turbulence separated them and they never saw each other again. For his part Cal was pushed out through a tube. He banged against the walls of the pipe and then returned to the torrent. It only took a few minutes until he got to the end of the piping, where the enormous stream of water was dispersed through the air in millions of drops that diffracted the light and formed a rainbow against the sky. Cal was trapped in one of the flying drops and ended up falling on to a mixture of materials that were mixed by mechanical arms. He couldn't understand what was happening. In his confusion the only thing that he thought was that these kinds of things happen with fate. So he accepted it and let himself be carried along by it.

17

A DARK ETERNITY

On the shores of Lake Kissimmee they were building a long wall made of reinforced concrete. Cement, sand and gravel were mixed with water before another pump sent them to be encased in an iron structure.

Cal moved around in the mixture trying to find an explanation for what was happening but no one could provide him with one. Then began what was for him a very rare process: the water molecules gradually lost their mobility and attracted him together with other calcium atoms to form a molecule of silicate. Within a short time calcium, silicate and oxygen atoms were bound in a solid, amorphous mass which, to be honest, did not have the order and the grace of those calcium carbonate crystals in the coral reef.

Fate determined that Cal would remain immobilized and in contact with the iron atoms, which were part of the metal structure of the reinforced concrete. Once more he became a slave, but this time in much tougher conditions, without the possibility of getting within reach of the outside world and a long way from the surface.

Next to him were Silicon and the others.

They spent the first forty years engaged in endless discussions. The immobility of the concrete invited them to talk and, as they had only recently met, everything was rather new. In particular Cal expanded his ideas about fate and Silicon recounted with copious details his extensive experience in a grain of sand. It was a good way of passing the time. In addition one of the oldest oxygen atoms, a born expert on the atmosphere, especially clouds and rain, entertained them every so often with the story of his incredible journeys. But even in this climate of understanding and predisposition to discussion, on the few occasions that Cal tried to introduce the subject of human beings, no-one understood or showed any interest in understanding. Eventually Cal grew tired of it and stopped bringing up the subject.

Over time the stories began to be told again and again. The enthusiasm of the early days had gone. Silicon, Oxygen, Cal himself - they all knew what the others were about to tell them. They tried to pretend that they were actually new stories and sometimes they changed a few details or altered the ending, but that didn't work. Boredom gradually infected Cal and eventually it overwhelmed him. The darkness was also to blame; it gave them no choices. All they could see was each other and, worse still, they were always in the same place: Silicon to the left, Oxygen to the right, and opposite were the iron atoms from the metal rod.

Not surprisingly one day they stopped talking to each other. Cal remembered the date very well: more than three hundred and forty two years had passed since he was sucked out of the lake. The heartache of not having anything to tell or listen to overcame him completely and there were no new experiences to enjoy. One extraordinary event of this period of his existence was a very intense tremor that shook the block of concrete for several hours before stillness returned once more. No-one could explain what had caused it.

In this latest isolation Cal realized that this was what immortality must be like, where each thought is the repetition of another one, and that one of yet another one, and that one in turn the portent of an infinite number of identical thoughts that would follow each other in the future. He thought that to be immortal would be like living in the human idea of hell which Francisco was so afraid of.

Every now and then, from one millennium to the next, they felt strange movements. They noticed that they were moving and were recovering the sensation of movement that they thought they had lost. In the millions of years of stillness they had only vibrated in their positions within the molecule. And of course for an atom, vibration or movement is not something that can be mistaken. After a few days everything returned to normality; they felt immobile again; for them nothing had changed.

During all this time of total darkness Cal suffered with the unbearable feeling of being immortal, until one fine day, unexpectedly, there appeared in the blackness a molecule of the kind that the air is made of, free of any ties, with its two oxygen atoms. After a few hours another one appeared, and then another, until finally there were thousands of them gliding around him. Some started to react chemically with the iron atoms in the rod that was opposite, so that it began to be covered in rust. The oxygen and nitrogen atoms entered through a crack that had formed in the block of cement, but Cal and his friends were too far away to be able to question the new arrivals – there were several centimeters between them. Just then, from one moment to the next, light appeared. Very faint, it was true, but it *was* light. At first Cal had no reaction, that is to say, no response: brightness was a concept he had forgotten, something buried in his memory for hundreds of millions of years. So he didn't take much notice; he thought that all old atoms must have that kind of hallucination. But the day after that brief glimmer he noticed that the light was coming almost imperceptibly from the end of the rod, where a small luminous dot was hesitating about whether to appear, as if it did not dare to enter the tomb.

Time passed. While Cal anxiously measured it again with his atomic clock, the dot disappeared and several hours later appeared once again. The cycle repeated itself: light and darkness at regular intervals. The experience was repeated for a week. The light appeared seven times and seven times it went away again, always at the same hour (of course, given the passage of time the days were longer and lasted nearly 29 hours). Cal was eventually convinced that this was the light of the Sun. At the same time the unexpected presence of oxygen and nitrogen molecules confirmed him in his thought that his tomb of cement was being breached by the air and the light.

Cal's conclusion coincided with an extraordinary occurrence: all of his friends seemed to wake up. Silicon emerged from his lengthy sleep and looked at Cal with curiosity, as if he had only just met him:

"Do you think it's the Sun?"

"Yes, replied Cal, "I'm sure it is."

Confirmation that it was indeed sunlight came a few weeks later, when via a long chain of atoms they received the important news: the block of concrete was breaking up.

The crucial moment had arrived. As torrents of water came in everywhere, the molecule of silicate, with Cal, Silicon and the other atoms, was dragged along the metal rod until they came out at the end and could abandon their lengthy imprisonment. Only when the current of water deposited them on to several millions of similar molecules, which formed a muddy mass on one side of the collapsed wall, did Cal realize that he had returned to the reality of the outside world.

18

NINE HUNDRED AND THIRTY MILLION YEARS LATER

Nine hundred and thirty four million years after the pump from the gigantic concrete-mixer had pulled Cal from the waters of Lake Kissimmee, a sea current set him down in the mud near an unfamiliar beach.

He was struck by the size of the waves. How come he was at the ocean's edge if the lake was situated more than a hundred kilometers from the Atlantic? He put this question to a nitrogen atom from an air molecule, while explaining that he had spent an incredibly long time in the concrete wall.

"During the millions of years that you mentioned, so many things have happened that I don't know where to start," said the nitrogen atom in an airy voice. There were huge movements in the Earth's crust, some continents joined up again and about two hundred and fifty million years ago a gigantic meteorite struck the Earth. Fortunately it was on the other side of the planet; it seemed like it would split the Earth in two. So you'd better believe it, what you can see is the ocean alright."

Cal said to himself: "The collision with the meteorite must have been that vibration that we felt in the concrete"...

Nitrogen went on:

"Your concrete wall disappeared millions of years ago: the earth tremors, the buffeting of the wind and the force of the ocean waves gradually demolished it until it was reduced to rubble."

Cal looked up and saw some small lumps of concrete scattered over the ground, with their edges smoothed from rubbing. The iron rods that were sticking out had been eaten away and covered with reddish oxide.

Nitrogen pointed to one which was almost round and was no more than three meters in diameter and said:

"That was your prison, Cal, and that's where you escaped from. You were unlucky; if you had remained near the surface when the wall was built your imprisonment would have lasted for a few thousand years and not the millions that you've told me about."

Cal sighed an atomic sigh and thought: "Such is fate, which is mysterious as well as immutable. I am merely an observer of its whims." But immediately he comforted himself with the thought that, since he couldn't predict the course of his fate, he was in the hands of chance.

The sensation of feeling himself to be free was so intense that he hadn't noticed the unbearable heat that enveloped them. Then he looked at the sky: the mist was rising from the sea and completely covered it.

"Nitrogen," said Cal, almost terrified, "you must understand that I spent more than nine hundred million years buried in that block of concrete. I only remember the first few hundred years, but afterwards time stopped for me. It is as if it had never passed. I lost the sense of many things: light, sounds, cold and heat. I don't even remember the temperature of the air!"

"I understand," said Nitrogen, with the consideration and solidarity typical of nitrogen atoms, "and I will try to help you."

During the conversation the waves were moving away from the shore. It was low tide. Cal thought that at least the Moon was still going round the Earth, as proved by the cycle of the tides. The mist was covering everything and the light from the Sun barely filtered through enough to let him know that it was still shining. He looked around him hoping to see plants and trees, but he only found a surface that was barren, yellowish, sad and lifeless.

He asked Nitrogen:

"Since you can see the Earth's surface when you are very high up in the atmosphere, tell me, what happened to the vegetation? Has the whole planet become a desert or just this area?"

"Your question is ancient history," replied Nitrogen. "It was about four hundred million years ago: the concentration of carbon dioxide in the air began to grow weaker. Without it, the trees and plants started to die, as together with water it was their basic food. You will know that chlorophyll and sunlight, via a process of photosynthesis, transformed them into carbohydrates. With the lack of carbon dioxide, that was the end of everything."

Cal thought back to the discussions in the sea, when he was a young atom and those who returned from their visits to the land told him about the mysteries of chlorophyll.

Cal was troubled by what Nitrogen told him; he thought of the years that Carbon had spent in the bark of a tree on the Caribbean coast and of the lush vegetation that surrounded him when Roberto was looking for his father's hometown in Asturias.

"Is this true? Plants, trees... they've all gone? Why did the carbon dioxide disappear from the air?"

"It's difficult to explain the process, at least for me, as I don't understand much about these things. But from what I've been told, as the temperature of the planet rose its virtual thermostat tried in vain to return to its previous equilibrium.

In order to achieve it absorbed a large part of the carbon dioxide from the atmosphere, making the most of the degradation of the silicates from the Earth's surface. But don't worry, all of their atoms, their carbons and oxygens, still exist. The only difference is that many of them went from freedom in the air to slavery in the silicates of the ground."

Cal thought: "The same as me, when in a flash I went from being a free ion to imprisonment in a silicate in concrete." He didn't feel like asking any more questions, but Nitrogen was feeling inspired and talkative and was trying, in a matter of minutes, to bring him up to date after a delay of nine hundred million years.

"I must tell you that later all the species of animals disappeared. It was a consequence of the gradual lack of food, since they stopped finding grass, grain and fruit, but it was also a consequence of the increase in temperature. The fish could tolerate up to forty degrees, mammals up to forty-five, and so on with the remaining living creatures. Of all of the species, algae and fungi lasted the longest."

All of the mortal creatures, as Cal and Carbon called them in their discussions in the reef, had disappeared.

Thinking about Carbon made him shudder; their friendship belonged to an important period in his existence. Then memories swept over him: the chain to pass on news,

Oxygen's ingenuity, the bulldozer that destroyed the reef, the escape up the chimney of the drying machine. It seemed as though everything happened yesterday. What became of Carbon and Oxygen?

Having listened to Nitrogen's explanation Cal felt that his idea of the planet was falling to pieces; it was disintegrating. He had returned to a new world which was completely different. In his memory he saw the desert-like image of Mars, which in his time with Roberto he never tired of watching. That's how the Earth seemed to him now, with the difference that it still had water, but ... for how much longer?

Nitrogen moved away, carried off by the wind, and Silicon acquired that isolation that had characterized him over the most recent millions of years, as if he couldn't manage to adapt to the new conditions, as if he longed for the immobility and the silence. So Cal was left on his own, and rummaging through his memory, he realized that he had returned to the external world at a tragic time: the Solar System was coming to an end.

He felt terribly sad. The most likely thing was that when this happened, it would also be the end for him. Yes, it was natural and he expected it. But however much he consoled himself with the firm belief that immortality would be unbearable, and despite all his efforts to change his position, he did not stop asking himself: Could this be my fate? In the rod alongside him a lot of water molecules were amusing themselves in the never-ending game of surrounding the ions; they protected them and they isolated them, playing the dual role of companions and custodians.

Cal turned to one of his neighbouring ions, a bromide:

"Were you with me in the tomb of cement?"

"No," Bromide replied, "I was in the sea; I was just one amongst the millions who went in to rescue you all."

"How long have you been in the sea?"

"I don't know, probably forever."

"A nitrogen atom that I met a moment ago explained to me how life on the planet disappeared. Could you tell me what happened to the humans? Did they disappear as well?"

"I don't know what you're talking about. What do you mean, 'humans'?"

Cal was nonplussed. How could one ion explain to another what humans were?

"I understand that you met living creatures: animals, fish."

"I remember something," said Bromide, "but that was a very long time ago. When the temperature started to go up they started disappearing. The only living things now are bacteria."

"Just bacteria?" said Cal, disappointed.

"Yes, just bacteria. I arrived on the planet more than four hundred and fifty million years ago and since my arrival I've never heard anyone talk about what you call humans."

"And the intelligent beings – did you meet them?"

"Not directly, but I know something about them. They inhabited the Earth until the planet's last normal day, and from then on they all started to emigrate to other parts of the galaxy."

"What do you mean – 'its last normal day'?"

"Don't you know? You must have forgotten – it's incredible what a block of concrete can do. They taught me when I was a child. Did you learn that the Sun was formed by the condensation of a hydrogen cloud and then it began to shine...?" Bromide hesitated: "You haven't forgotten that, have you?"

"No, even a hundred year-old atom knows that. Go on."

"Well, the intensity of the sunlight increased until suddenly the brightness stabilized and that's how it stayed for billions of years. But the Sun is going to go out. We estimate that, measured from its birth until its death, it will have a life of about eleven billion years. By 'death' I mean its end as a star. Before that it will start to increase its size and its brightness..."

"Is that what the increase in temperature that I can notice is due to?"

"I don't know, but I imagine so. As I was saying... the Sun will increase in size and brightness until it turns into an enormous sphere, a Red Giant that will entrap the closest planets – Mercury, Venus, maybe the Earth. Then it will go through different stages, until it turns into a white dwarf, like so many others that can be seen in the sky."

"And 'the last normal day'? I still don't understand."

"The last normal day for the Earth was when the brightness of the Sun started to change," declared Bromide. "It's like a milestone in the history of the planet. The intelligent beings knew that from that day on the conditions for survival on Earth were going to get worse. The day was only of symbolic value because they reckoned that it would take centuries before the change would have an effect on them. They started to look for a planet in the galaxy that was like the Earth but which orbited around a much younger star than the Sun. It was a way of guaranteeing a new home for billions of years. In order to avoid great changes in their way of life the new planet had to have more or less the same mass and gravitational pull as the Earth, water in a liquid state and an atmosphere with a reasonable percentage of oxygen, as well as an ambient temperature that kept similar values to those to which they were accustomed. In short, they set about looking for a planet like the Earth but a lot younger."

"And did they find it?"

"It took them hundreds of years to find it..." Bromide answered calmly. "When they did so, they were full of hope and sent a mission to confirm what their observations and calculations had predicted. By that time they had spaceships for interstellar voyages that travelled at great speed. To give you an idea, it took them barely a hundred years for a return journey to Alpha Centauri."

"How were they powered?" Cal asked, very intrigued.

"They said it was something connected with anti-matter, but I'm not sure. When the explorers reached the unknown planet after a journey of nearly a hundred and fifty years, they reported that the conditions they had found were those predicted by their calculations and direct observations. And the most important thing was that organic life recently started to develop there. They only found small, single cell organisms. That finally convinced them that they had made the right choice."

"So they left the Earth?"

"Yes, but they emigrated in a very orderly manner. In about twenty thousand years all of the intelligent beings reached their new home in the Milky Way."

"And the living creatures that inhabited the Earth at that time?"

"They left them behind; they couldn't take them with them... When the exodus was over, the Sun had not yet undergone great changes."

Cal was speechless and once again felt himself to be outside of time. He was tormented by the fact that Bromide didn't know about human beings. What he was telling him about intelligent beings had happened more than five hundred million years earlier, and according to him humans no longer existed by then!

19

THE TEACHINGS OF A NOBLE ATOM

Cal was bewildered and felt that Bromide was exaggerating his story somewhat. He even wondered whether the account of the exodus from the Earth was pure fantasy. He couldn't get used to so many changes. For a good while he missed the block of concrete, where fate seemed to be frozen, but then he told himself that he must adapt again. Gradually he managed to do so, until one day he once more felt that time was passing again.

When the level of the sea rose because of the tide, Cal could feel the temperature of the water increasing day by day. Would it one day turn into an enormous cauldron? The mist from the steam prevented him from seeing the sky, so he missed the spectacle of the distant stars and the setting sun with the clouds painted in all the colours of the rainbow.

He spent several years like this without making sense of things and was in the midst of this feeling of nostalgia when, by chance, he met Argon.

Argon was a noble atom. He belonged to one of the six families – together with those of helium, neon, radon, xenon and krypton – that do not share their electrons with other atoms, in other words, they do not allow themselves to combine to form molecules. Their nobility lies in not mixing with the other plebeian elements. They keep themselves apart and in addition, with the exception of the helium atoms, they are rare and few and far between: less than one per cent of the atoms that make up the Earth's atmosphere belong to this species.

It was a great occasion for Cal to meet Argon at that time in his existence. He had a bit of a complex; here he was, a humble atom, consorting with an aristocrat. Nevertheless he thought Argon was terrific; he was a great traveller who had seen from the air all of the changes that had occurred on the planet during Cal's imprisonment over hundreds of millions of years.

In their first conversation, after telling him that story, he begged:

"Argon, please talk to me about the sky. I haven't seen it again."

"You wouldn't recognise it," Argon replied. "The Sun has grown in size and is much bigger than the one you knew because it has started the process of extinction. It's strange; it's losing its strength but every day it gives out more energy. The water in the sea will eventually boil."

"Tell me more, tell me more!" begged Cal.

"The image of the sky is different from what you remember. The stars appear distant because the Universe has continued to expand... Do you remember the galaxies? Now they are scarcely visible; you can only see the stars of the Milky Way, which are ever more distant, except for the Andromeda galaxy, which is getting closer, and the other ones that are nearer to us, amongst them Sagittarius. The old star Sirius, whose brightness made so many others look pale, no longer exists; some seventy million years after the concrete trapped you it turned into a Red Giant, then expelled almost all of its matter into space and is now an insignificant White Dwarf left to wander aimlessly. What happened to it is the same thing that will happen with the Sun."

Cal realised that he was in the company of a knowledgeable and serious atom who had at his disposal an enormous amount of information. He was excited by the thought that Argon could unravel the mystery that had always preoccupied him.

So he didn't hesitate and came out with the question:

"Did you manage to get to know human beings?"

Argon looked at him with curiosity. What could this lowly atom of calcium know about such a strange and remote subject?

"Not directly, I was never in contact, but I did hear about them. This was a very long time ago…"

Somewhat relieved, Cal ventured to recount his experience. He began with his early years in the sea, with the beginnings of life, the first molecules of amino acids, proteins, crustaceans… And so he went on, stage by stage of evolution, ending with humans and his experiences with Francisco and Roberto. When he finished his account, which Argon listened to in surprise, he added:

"I understand that humans have not inhabited the Earth for long time, but I should like to know if the species died out like the dinosaurs or if it managed to survive. Bromide, an ion that I met a short time ago, told me a bit about the great exodus of the intelligent beings after the 'last normal day', but he couldn't remember what had become of human beings."

"I know a few tales about the human race," said Argon, "but as you know, such tales owe a lot to fantasy. Every time I tell them I add something, and that's what everyone probably does, so that I can't guarantee that they are true stories. Given what you say about your conversation with Bromide, I gather that you know that humans were supplanted by much more intelligent beings…"

"Yes," Cal quickly responded, "and I even know when the process started. It was a long time ago, at the beginning of the twenty-first century in their numbering system. I also know that it all began with a machine that they had invented: the computer."

"I'll tell you what I think," said the noble atom. "Human beings represented a stage, but only a stage, in the evolution of intelligence on the Earth. The next one was that of the Artificial Intelligences. Humans called them artificial because they had created them, but the fact is that these artificial beings were their successors in the evolutionary chain. You have to recognise that from the moment when they discovered how to reproduce, they stopped being artificial. That's the fundamental thing. In their turn, they also changed a lot. What I mean is… the beings that started to leave the Earth on 'the last normal day' had nothing to do with their ancestors. Don't forget that they had evolved over millions of years."

"Human beings also evolved," said Cal.

"Yes, but the limitations of their molecular biology, based on the chemistry of carbon, didn't allow them to evolve further, and in any case they had no need to. The artificial beings did their thinking for them and they solved all their problems. The size of the human brain grew very little compared to the development achieved by the Artificial Intelligences, and in addition the slowness of the human neurons was a terrible liability. Imagine, barely two hundred contacts per second! I know that they tried to make progress with neural implants, but they didn't help much. Ultimately the speed of change of other beings left them behind forever. But there's something more important that you appear to be unaware of. When were you trapped in the concrete wall?"

"In the middle of the twenty-fourth century in the human numbering system."

"A hundred and fifty or two hundred centuries after you began your imprisonment the planet started to freeze and a glacial period began that lasted for more than eighty thousand years. The glaciers ended by covering half of the Earth's surface and the environmental conditions of the rest of the planet changed completely."

"The same as in the time of the cavemen," Cal whispered.

Argon appeared not to hear him and went on:

"The human population was very numerous and there were migrations of whole countries towards the equatorial regions. The intelligent beings could not control the process and so they allowed the inevitable to happen: worldwide destruction and death. Wars and famine resulted in the disappearance of the greater part of the human race. The colonies on the Moon and Mars, which until then had been seen as inhospitable places, turned into a paradise. The same thing happened with the rest of the Earth's biomass: less than ten per cent of its plants and animals managed to survive. But when the glacial period came to an end, the worst happened: in less than ten years the great mass of ice was transformed into torrents of water that devastated everything and changed the surface of the planet. The intelligent beings also suffered intensely. Many of them were destroyed and a large part of their work disappeared. The reconstruction process took them thousands of years."

Cal was dumbfounded. He didn't want to hear what Argon was telling him, although his memory of the effects of the Ice Age at the beginning of human civilisation eventually convinced him. He thought: 'but at that time there were very few humans...'. On the other hand he knew that at the end of that period of thousands of years the Earth's surface had changed in appearance: the Norwegian fjords, the Great Lakes of North America and many other geographical accidents had been created during the thawing of the glaciers.

Cal could not hide his concern:

"Anyway, Argon, why don't you tell me about what happened to those who survived the catastrophe? Tell me one of those tales that you know…"

"First I'll tell you the one that seems the most optimistic. The problem with this story is that it comes from someone I know, an argon who was arrogant and whose fantasy knew no limits. According to him there was a moment in which a few humans managed to integrate their brain with the artificial intelligence that they themselves had created, and so a new species came about, which they called 'transhuman'. These individuals kept the personality and qualities that identified them as humans, but their intelligence, which was less biological and more artificial each day, reached extraordinary levels of ability. These beings, to a certain extent successors to and preservers of humans (hence the term transhumans), were the Artificial Intelligences which we have referred to. But from what I have been told about their appearance, I am sure that you would not recognise in them your old friends Francisco and Roberto."

Cal tried to conceal the joy that that tale had aroused in him and asked the noble atom to tell him another one.

"I remember a very sad one, but it's not awful," said Argon kindly. "The story goes that after the great destruction the human race was going downhill so much that humans ceased to be useful to the intelligent beings. The robots carried out all the tasks that civilisation required of them, even more efficiently and at a lower cost than humans. So they decided to finish with them. It wasn't a cruel end; they just stopped them from reproducing. So in less than two hundred years the human race died out by itself, without any need for violence."

"Do you remember any other, happier tales?" asked Calcium.

"Yes, there are lots of them. This is most entertaining one I know about the fate of your humans, the survivors, because it nicely combines the scientific with the epic. Are you ready? The story goes that the intelligent beings were protecting humans by controlling their reproduction and that gradually they were selecting the fittest. When they started to emigrate after the 'last normal day' they took with them frozen human embryos. Humans, with their temporal and psychological limitations, wouldn't have survived the journey. According to this tale, the human race that you knew still exists on another planet in the Milky Way, probably as a curiosity under the protection of much more intelligent beings who live much longer. As for those who were abandoned here after the emigration, I gather that there weren't many of them and they were spread over the Earth's surface in about ten space stations, as well as in a few colonies on the Moon and on

Mars. Their dependency over millions of years would have made them incapable of dealing with the environmental difficulties by themselves. They were able to survive for a limited period – perhaps a few thousand years. Then the species began to die out before finally disappearing.

"So I lost the bet," muttered Cal.

"What bet?"

"Never mind, it doesn't matter now."

Argon looked at Cal with a mixture of tenderness and sadness.

"I suggest that you forget about humans," he said to him. "I understand that they've been one of your favourite subjects, but that was all so long ago that it doesn't make sense any more. I think it's time we thought about ourselves. Human beings were on the Earth for a hundred million years, or if you like at the very most five hundred million. Do you know how much that amount of time means set against the Earth's existence? Less than five per cent of its history... That's nothing!"

"But they were the first rational beings on the planet."

"On this planet," Argon corrected.

"Yes, of course, on this planet... The only one I was able to get to know."

"I suggest we spend one of these days talking about the evolution of intelligence on the rest of the planets in the Milky Way. You'll note that I'm restricting it to our galaxy, which is the one that I know. I can't begin to imagine what the result would be if we could find out what happens in the other billions of galaxies in the Universe."

Cal replied:

"I think that more or less the same thing must happen in all the galaxies."

"I agree," Argon responded, "so you can imagine how many civilisations there must be right now. But it's possible that not all developments are the same. If we confine ourselves to the Earth, I admit that your human beings represented an important stage in its evolution – they were pioneers – but you must accept that the beings that followed them in that chain were infinitely more rational and intelligent."

"How will they be getting on in the new planet?" asked Cal, aware that humans would also be there.

"Quite well, I suppose. I can't imagine that they wouldn't. But Cal, please forget about them and come back to our times. From what I can see in my wanderings on the clouds, the Sun is getting bigger and brighter. The strength of its radiation is remarkable – have you noticed how the temperature is going up? I think that very soon all the water in the sea will evaporate."

"And with it my hopes of becoming an ion again," said Cal in a quiet voice.

Argon appeared not to notice his comment.

"Let's imagine how the Earth will come to an end and us with it… Remember what they taught us when we were little? 'As the Sun burns up its hydrogen and the nuclear reaction slows down, it will start to inflate like a balloon and will turn into a Red Giant like so many similar stars that we can see in the sky' … Well, that process has started. Our planet will melt like an ice-cube in the fire and from then on we will be in fate's hands."

Cal remembered old Phosphorus, his companion in Bream's bone and Francisco's shoulder-blade, whom he hadn't seen again since the day that they were separated during the tumble on a Cantabrian beach. He said to himself: 'the memory knows nothing of time; it piles up reminiscences and makes us relive them all together, simultaneously, in the present.' In Cal's memory Phosphorus appeared, telling his story about the formation of the Earth when it was still a mass of stellar dust revolving around the Sun. How strange! Now he would be a witness of the end: two billion years had passed in a flash. His memory and his imagination enabled him to fuse the two acts into one, timelessly.

Alongside Cal thousands of very rare and identical molecules were piled up in an area of no more than a cubic millimetre. It was the first time that Cal realised that they were there. Each molecule contained two atoms of selenium, one of copper, one of indium and the last of gallium. Except for the copper atom the others were totally unknown, strange and incredible, but there was no doubt that they were atoms.

Just as Cal was about to question them, the selenium atom, which was nearest, got in before him.

"I imagine that you will be wondering who we are and what we're doing here."

Cal did not deny his interest.

"We are a molecule that human beings who used to live on Earth synthesised a very long time ago," Selenium informed him. "I imagine that you will have heard of them..."

Cal nodded in silence.

"They manufactured us because we turned out to be very useful. We have an amazing capacity to transform the light from the Sun into electrical energy. They used us to build what they called solar panels, which at their peak covered a substantial part of the planet's surface. When the human race was wiped out we were left abandoned. This happened more than nine hundred million years ago. Now we have turned into atomic waste, I know; it's the wear and tear of the centuries. The movements of the Earth's crust, the impact of the meteorite that almost wiped us from space, the winds, the battering, they all completely destroyed the panels, and we were amongst the millions of pieces that flew everywhere. That's how we came to end up here."

Fascinated, Cal suddenly remembered having seen some solar panels on the side of the airport that they were building for the underwater hotel.

"Were you on a tiny island to the north of the Bahamas?"

"No, we were installed in northern Florida, near the coast," replied Selenium. "I think the place was covered by the sea. You know, I was very interested in your conversation with Argon. I didn't want to interrupt you; it didn't seem like a good idea. Now that he's gone I can admit to you that I find Argon's aristocratic air a bit intimidating."

"Oh, come on… he's an atom like the rest of us," Cal declared. "What are you trying to say?"

"Nothing in particular. I'd like us to think things out together. Everything that all of you have learnt and that you are repeating now are the conclusions that older atoms than us have reached from their observations of other planetary systems similar to our own. I want to stress the word 'similar' because despite the fact that there are billions of stars like the Sun, I don't believe that there are two identical systems in the Universe. If they are not identical, then there's no reason why their end should be the same, either."

"Go on," said Cal, encouraged by this reasoning.

"I have been on the Earth since its formation. For centuries I was wandering in space around the Sun, which was starting to turn into a star."

"Did you know Phosphorus?"

"Who?"

"Sorry, Selenium, please carry on with your explanation."

"When I was going round in space I was one of the disciples of Helium, who was a very wise atom and had an enormous amount of experience. He was one of the few old helium atoms left, one of the ones that were born with the Universe. He explained that we were taking part in the formation of a planetary system, how it would evolve and what its possible end might be."

Just then Argon returned and sat listening. Selenium addressed both of them:

"What you imagine will happen is the most likely, that's for sure, but Helium also told us that he had been able to study some exceptional cases. The probability that the Solar System was one of these exceptions is one in a hundred thousand, but the possibility exists."

When he heard that, a picture clearly emerged from amongst Cal's memories: Joaquín saying to Francisco one afternoon in the Barrio Alto: 'If only we had the same luck as that guy who won the jackpot in the Christmas lottery'… The odds that Selenium was giving were more or less the same: one in a hundred thousand.

Argon kept silent and Selenium went on:

"Helium explained to me that in those exceptional cases the path of the Sun could cross with that of another star and that if they are close enough the planetary systems of the two stars would be altered. If this happened the Earth would have two possibilities: either it gets embedded into the Sun or it gets fired off like a bullet through the Milky Way."

"What else did you learn from Helium?" asked Cal, eager for more new ideas.

"They've calculated that the Andromeda galaxy and ours are approaching each other at a speed of three hundred kilometres per second, so the distance that separates them today could be covered in only two billion years."

"By then the Sun will have swallowed us up," said Cal, "and we will have ceased to exist."

Argon, who was impressed by the deductive ability of the plebeian Cal and the rare Selenium, withdrew without saying a word, although he thought about going through the blanket of fog in order to study the sky. It was a good opportunity, as it was night-time and he could take a careful look at the stars.

A very light breeze was blowing, but it was strong enough for Argon to let himself be swept along, initially at ground level until he was over the sea, where a puff of water vapour pushed him upwards. He passed through the mist and the heavens appeared, blacker than he had ever seen them before. The huge Sun had disappeared. There was a new Moon and darkness reigned. He had the same thought that he always had at that hour: How different the sky looked compared to the days of his youth! Only a few, pale stars.... You couldn't make out the nebular ones... Where was Orion now, the birthplace of so many stars?

He wandered around for a while and tried to see if there were any changes that would indicate something new for his new friend, the Cal atom, when another argon atom that was travelling alongside him asked:

"What do you think those two bright dots are that you can see near the horizon?"

"Where? I can't see them," said Argon.

"Down there. Perhaps that mountain top is in your way... A little to the right."

Argon was an expert in Cosmography.

"They're two stars. It's a binary system."

"What?" his fellow atom asked, rather puzzled.

"Many stellar systems in the Universe are made up of two stars that revolve around a common system of gravity. A significant number of these systems have planets like those of the Solar System. We experts call these inhabitants of the Universe binary systems."

The other Argon tried to imagine what it would be like at sunrise and sunset on a planet with two suns, but his intelligence wouldn't stretch that far and he didn't dare to ask.

Argon went on:

"They are two stars that are very close to each other and travel together. But I confess that this is the first time that I've seen them. The only explanation I can think of is that they are stars that belong to the dwarf galaxy of Sagittarius. As you know the Milky Way has been gobbling it up for more than a hundred and fifty million years... Argon checked the time, did a few triangulations using other points of reference and said to the passing argon: "If we come back to the same place in a year's time we'll be able to note if they've moved and in what direction. Now let's get back to the surface;" he was anxious to tell Cal and Silenium about what they had found.

They tried to find a downward draught of air and having been given a shove by nitrogen atoms and a few others they went through the cloud cover once more. Argon headed for the coast. The rubble from the old concrete wall helped him to find his way.

Once they were back Cal greeted him with a joke:

"How did Mr Noble get on in his excursion through the atmosphere?"

"It's obvious that the atoms who can't fly are just jealous; what's more, their jokes don't take off," replied Argon. "You'll never guess what I've discovered. It was just by chance."

Cal and Selenium looked at him in expectation.

"I saw two stars, a binary system that you couldn't see before from Earth."

Selenium's eyes lit up:

"One in a hundred thousand," he whispered.

"I'll come back in a year's time to see if the system has moved and if so in which direction."

"That's not necessary," replied Selenium.

"What do you mean it's not necessary?" Argon felt annoyed. Sometimes he let slip that air of superiority that was part of his lineage.

"If you didn't see them in the sky before but now you can, it means that these two stars are getting closer to the Solar System. Anyway it doesn't seem a bad idea to me if you come back to see them in order to confirm their trajectory."

The news spread from atom to atom in an endless chain and caused an unusual commotion. Everyone awaited Argon's new measurements.

Three months after this episode, with still another nine to go before the figures were due to be checked, Cal made a suggestion to Argon:

"Why don't you go and have a look now? Don't you think you might notice something?"

"I said a year and a year it'll be. And don't worry, Cal, we atoms aren't like that. I think that human beings have passed on to you some of their failings."

It wasn't a crazy notion, although with regard to the similarity with human behaviour, Argon had no reason to be jealous of Calcium.

When the year was up, Argon flew up again in good time. The argon atom with the telescopic vision, as well as thousands of onlookers, went with him. The plan was to get to the same place and stay there until the designated time.

Argon got his bearings with the other stars and the mountain top that had already served as a point of reference. He checked the time and when he looked towards the place where he reckoned the stars would be, he realised that he didn't need the telescopic vision of his friend: the brightness was several times greater compared to a year earlier. Yes, Selenium was right: the pair of stars were approaching the Solar System at great speed.

When they returned the news shook all the atoms of the group and then started to spread in all directions. They suffered an attack of nerves – atomic ones, of course. It was fortunate that Selenium was with them. His wisdom surprised them and served to calm them down. Silicon, the most frightened of all, started to say that there was going to be a collision between the stars and they would be swallowed up in the disaster.

Selenium didn't bat an eyelid:

"I'll tell you what's going to happen. When the distance between the Sun and the approaching stars gets to a certain point, their gravitational fields will start to pull on each other. The first one to change course will be Jupiter. Its displacement will be catastrophic for the Earth: we'll either fall towards the

Sun or we'll be thrown into outer space like a meteor and we'll cease to orbit around the Sun. In the latter case we'll be free, independent, alone. Our direction will be unknown and unpredictable. In short, we'll embark on a journey that will be out of this world. The Earth will become a spaceship and we will be its passengers."

Cal saw the rail of the boat clearly in his memory. Francisco was winding around his wrist the weighted line loaded with hooks, using clams as bait. At that moment the line broke and the weight went flying into the sky like an arrow. Francisco watched it disappear out of sight. The lead weight that was the Earth would fly in the same way. The approaching stars would be responsible for breaking the line that kept it bound to the Sun.

20

JOURNEY TO INFINITY

The appearance of the two approaching stars caused a stir amongst the atoms. While Cal tried to keep calm, Gallium and others calculated what might happen to the Earth. Everyone awaited their conclusions anxiously. That was when they were surprised by a strange sound. The temperature of the sea was increasing day by day and the dissolved gases were escaping into the atmosphere. The noise that they could hear was that produced water before it starts to boil. The spectacle presented by the sea was like something out of Dante, with millions of bubbles breaking its surface.

Cal had never witnessed anything like it in his existence before. He looked questioningly at Selenium before stating:

"I think that before your stars arrive to save us we'll be roasted by the Sun."

Selenium turned to Gallium in search of a reply, but he didn't dare to ask him anything as he looked more anxious than Selenium was.

"Poor fish…" was the only thing that Silicon managed to say.

"Don't be silly, Silicon, they all died millions of years ago," Selenium replied. The water temperature made the sea uninhabitable a long time ago."

Four years later the whole area next to the old coast had been turned into a salt marsh. The water had evaporated and the dissolved salts had been deposited on what had been the sea bed. Cal reckoned that there were almost forty kilos of salt for every thousand litres of water, and he couldn't help thinking of the first time that he had known what it was to feel calm: on an enormous, flat rock on the water's edge, in that pool that had been transformed into a small white patch when all the water molecules had abandoned him so as to travel in the air.

Every so often, accompanied by several thousands of atoms, Argon went up into the atmosphere to check on the movement of the binary stars. The number of astronomer-atoms grew day by day and on their return they passed on the collected data to Gallium so that he could amend his calculations. It was a race against time. They were betting on the stars, although they weren't sure if the gravitational pull of the travellers would save them or if it would hasten their destruction. The mist covered everything; the atmosphere which had been heated by the growing radiation of the Sun was capable of storing an incredible amount of water vapour. The atoms that were still on the ground felt as though they were floating in a cloud.

As if someone were setting alight an enormous fire and then putting it out again, the sea seemed to be at boiling point during the day but quietened down at night and started the process again in the middle of the morning.

A long time passed in this way, and the anxiety amongst the atoms about the outcome showed no signs of coming to an end.

One day, when everyone was waiting for the noise of the sea around midday, there was nothing to be heard. From then on the waters gradually became quieter, with only the waves disturbing the surface.

Everyone looked at Selenium in search of an explanation, but he was engaged in a discussion with Gallium, Copper and Indium – his companions in the molecule – and didn't notice them. After a while Selenium looked up, paused at length (perhaps to make the most of the moment) and addressing everyone around him, said in a solemn tone:

"I can confirm that the Earth has started to leave the Solar System…"

The atoms were stunned. Selenium, who handled the apprehension very well, concluded:

"In a few years time, the old planet that we love so much will have turned into an enormous asteroid."

The delight of the atoms was beyond description. One of the most excited was Silicon, and even Argon himself lost his normal composure, as he began to shout:

"I discovered the binary stars!"

In keeping with his noble habits, the argon with the telescopic vision did not contradict him.

Cal wanted to celebrate, but the fear of remaining bound in the silicate molecule made him feel uneasy.

"When will I be able to feel free once and for all?" he whispered.

"Soon," said Silenium.

Cal was unconvinced and asked:

"Why do you say that?"

"Because that's how it will be. Gallium's calculations can't be wrong. The attraction of the binary stars has already disrupted the orbit of Jupiter and now almost all of the other planets, except Venus and Mercury, will find their paths altered. The process has already started for the Earth: it will continue to orbit round the Sun for a while, but will get further and further away until it gets launched out into space. As we are moving away from the star that provides us with heat and light, the temperature, which has already started to fall, will continue to do so, as will the amount of light. I'm afraid that you are going to have to get used to the darkness again, my dear friend. When the temperature goes down far enough, this whole enormous mass of water vapour that covers the planet will condense and turn into rain."

"And then what?"

"Water will cover the Earth and you'll go back to the sea. And as you say, you can take it from me that the premise will be fulfilled: every calcium atom that returns to the sea will, sooner or later, turn into an ion."

Cal had come to like Selenium; he was a terrific atom. It would be very hard for him to have to leave him.

"What'll happen to you?"

"I don't know; I've never been in the water."

"Did your teacher, Helium, never explain to you? I don't want to depress you but in my long experience in the sea I never came across a Selenium atom," said Cal with candour.

Gallium, Selenium's molecular companion, rarely intervened in these conversations, but on this occasion, perhaps realising that the others knew nothing about the subject, began:

"Selenium, almost the whole of your time on the planet you spent bound to a mineral, until one day – I imagine it was historic for you – when humans extracted you from the ground, you found yourself separated from the other atoms and for a while you were pure selenium. Then they combined you with me, Indium and Copper, and the result was this nice molecule that we share."

"Gallium, you're telling my story… I already know it."

"But it would seem that you don't remember much chemistry and you don't understand that there are other seleniums with different histories from yours. You ought to know that there's selenic acid and also the selenates, and many of them are soluble in water. I also agree with Cal that you lot in the sea are an oddity."

"What do you mean?"

"I mean that if we end up in the sea anything could happen to us, including getting split up and you turning into an ion selenate…"

Six months after Cal, Gallium and Selenium held this conversation, they were in almost total darkness. It was difficult to tell night from day. Then it started to rain. First a few hesitant drops, then a downpour, and finally a deluge. For several weeks the water ran constantly over the Earth's surface, collecting in the most low-lying areas before turning into torrent after countless torrent.

Cal remained in the bottom of a valley where one of these currents would pass. Suddenly, when he saw the wall of water, earth and rocks approaching, he said resolutely to Selenium:

"Let's try to keep together; I'd like to share some time in the water with you and your friends."

Argon had disappeared. They imagined him above the storm, far away in space, watching the Earth moving away from the Sun.

Cal went round and round in that torrent of rainwater that dragged him out to the sea. When he entered the water there was a long struggle with his companions in the calcium silicate molecule (Silicon and the oxygen atoms) but the water molecules helped him and some days later he was able to free himself from his bonds and turn into an ion again.

Immediately he started to look for Selenium. He tried to reach the bottom, assuming that the molecule of selenium, copper, gallium and indium, which is insoluble in water, would have landed on the sea bed together with other molecules like theirs that formed the microscopic particle of the old solar panel. There was hardly any light, but recognising that he would have to get used to that, he went down even further. Near the bottom the darkness was impenetrable. Cal thought: 'From now on I ought to forget about my optical vision and I'll have to rely on my other atomic attributes.' He realised that he was again experiencing the sensations of his childhood when he was travelling through space in the stellar cloud. He searched for a long time but in vain. Then, having given up all hope, he abandoned the search. He was heart-broken.

The sea water was slowly getting colder. There were lots of thermal currents, some coming up from the hot water at the bottom, others coming down with the cold water on the surface. Cal let himself be carried along by an upward current, and a few metres from the surface he heard alongside him a familiar voice, although it was somewhat distorted by the water molecules in between:

"How are you feeling, Cal? I see you've managed to get free again. You're looking good."

It was a heavy ion, like a sulphate.

"I'm sorry, I don't recognise you."

"Look at me carefully," said the other one.

"Selenium!" exclaimed Calcium. "You're in disguise! I didn't recognise you!"

"Gallium was right, selenic acid does exist. Now I'm an ion like you. Not as independent, of course; I'm a selenate ion. I'm accompanied by four oxygens. I can see that I'm destined to stay with them for a long time."

"What happened? What about Gallium, Copper, Indium...?"

"They're all okay, don't worry. And don't ask me how it happened; it was complicated but it turned out alright. The important thing is that I now know what it means for an atom to feel like an ion."

The oxygen atoms that formed the selenate ion remained silently hostile.

Selenium explained to Cal:

"Ever since they joined me in the ion they haven't said a word to me. I don't think they like the new situation.

"What will happen now with the Earth?" asked Cal.

No-one spoke.

The silence, which lasted for minutes, was broken by a deep voice that said:

"I have lots of experience in inter-stellar space, and in the atmosphere and the sea of this unimportant planet, and I am an ancient observer of the evolution of the Universe, so I can explain to you what's going to happen to us."

'It can't be,' thought Cal, 'it would be an incredible coincidence.' But there was no doubt about it; it was indeed Hydrogen, his old counsellor. It occurred to him that the explanation as to why he had met up in this place with Hydrogen after so long was the same as the unexpected encounter by Elvira and Roberto with the suicide bomber in the plane: an almost infinite succession of causal events, unpredictable but predetermined, which come together in a single spot and proclaim either joy or tragedy.

Still in the same molecule of water. His single electron was revolving as usual, vigorous and strong. Time had stood still for Hydrogen. At that moment he could not help thinking nostalgically about Phosphorus and his 'brother' calcium, his old Cantabrian friends, and Oxygen and Carbon, lying still by his side in the coral reef. Would fate ever bring them together again?

Hydrogen went on:

"Don't ask me now how we came to end up in this place; I'll tell you one day. I hope also that you'll tell me if you had the chance to enter a human being and how you got on with that brief experience… Were you fixed to a bone? Wait, don't tell me now, we'll have time to talk. Right now you'll be wondering what's going to happen in the future. I'll tell you…"

What he was hoping for from Hydrogen the teacher was an explanation of what the consequences would be of moving away from the Sun, some of which Selenium had already told them. Hydrogen, who up to that point had only been talking to Cal, realised that the other atoms were also interested and addressed them all as he went on:

"It'll be about another four billion years before the Sun turns into a Red Giant and its existence comes to an end. But as a star it's now useless. It's fortunate that we were saved by the binary stars. When the Sun reaches its final stage its diameter will increase hundreds of times and it will trap its nearest planet, Mercury. The mass of hydrogen that made up the Sun is becoming exhausted; what served as its fuel for billions of years has turned into helium. In the future the Sun will undergo contractions and expansions, it will throw out into space a large part of its matter, and finally it will turn into a white dwarf. It will be reduced to the size of the Earth. Its fate will be to wander through the Milky Way forever."

Cal anxiously interrupted him:

"Don't take offence, Hydrogen; I wasn't asking about the fate of the Sun, but about the fate of the Earth."

The old atom said to himself: 'That Cal is the same as ever; he hasn't changed one bit.'

"I was just getting to that when you interrupted me...
The Earth, with us on it," Hydrogen went on, "is flying
through space on an unknown course. For several centuries
we'll be within the Milky Way, but after that I don't know. In
fact no-one knows, although I imagine that fate has already
decided. The only certain thing is that the temperature of our
planet will continue to go down; it will fall to a few degrees
above absolute zero and we'll have no light. The only light
that will guide us on our journey will be the light from the
stars."

"What will happen with the sea?"

"Its surface will freeze over, Cal, but that'll take a few
years yet. Then in, let's say, a million years more, almost the
whole of the sea will be a mass of ice, except in those regions
where nuclear fission, which will still be active in the centre of
the Earth, produces the necessary heat to prevent it. I think
that we'll soon have to look for one of those places to settle in,
so that we can keep our mobility."

Cal felt that it was time to rise to the surface. It was
only a few metres away. He let himself float upwards until he
could see the sky. But that wasn't the image that surprised
him; it was the water – with scarcely a wave, the surface was
barely rippled by a very gentle breeze. There was no longer
any night and day, nor dawns and dusks. The Sun, which was

a lot further away, seemed small, an unreal, yellowish image. Then, just before he submerged himself again, he discovered something strange in the sky, as if a cloud were blurring the weak image of the stars.

"What's that?" Cal asked a hydrogen atom from one of the water molecules that surrounded him.

"It's the first time that I've seen it, but no doubt it's something that's in space on our route between the Sun and infinity."

The other hydrogen atom from the same molecule, who was more alert than his companion – or at least better informed – explained:

"It's very common to find them in space. They're the remains of matter expelled by old stars like the Sun or by the explosion of some Supernova. They call it stardust."

Cal felt himself go faint, bewildered by the memory of his early years: the cloud of stellar dust, his coming together with Oxygen, the wayward asteroid, that cylinder full of craters that didn't want to take them, the descent on to the pale blue planet.

He hounded the hydrogen atom with his question:

"Do you think we're going towards it?"

"Yes, but don't get anxious, it's only dust. We'll go straight past it without even realising it."

Cal didn't want to carry on looking and hurriedly dived down; he needed to tell Selenium what was happening. To his surprise he found Selenium talking with Silicon, his companion in the concrete block, as usual bound to the silicate ion.

Cal greeted Silicon rather coldly (nine hundred million years in his company were weighing him down) and he turned to Selenium:

"We're about to go through a stellar dust cloud. We're going to come across a countless number of very young atoms."

Selenium showed some interest:

"Are we really going to cross paths with them?"

"I think so."

"That'll be marvellous," said Silenium. "Let's put out the red carpet for them."

Cal looked at the water molecules that accompanied him, and then warned their atoms:

"I understand that chemical forces compel you to act and I know that I cannot prevent it. But I give you this warning: if a molecule of calcium oxide happens to fall near you and you feel that you have to attack it, before you do so you should remember that that molecule is made up of atoms like yourselves. Be sensible and don't behave like animals!"

The atoms looked at him in surprise. They didn't understand why he felt the need to be so forceful.

The Earth had turned into a wandering planet, a globe twelve thousand kilometres in diameter travelling through outer space. It went through the cloud of stellar dust without any sign of change, just as the cigar-shaped asteroid had done when Cal encountered it in his childhood. However, for the atoms, molecules and particles in the cloud it was a remarkable event. Cal and Selenium, together with the oxygen atoms of the selenate ion, got close to the surface so that they could watch the spectacle. They didn't want to miss it. It was really impressive: countless passengers from the stardust were trapped by the Earth.

As he approached a group of new arrivals, without finding any calcium oxide, Cal breathed a sigh of relief. The scene of carnage had been avoided.

They all noticed the large number of iron and carbon particles that were travelling in the cloud. They fell on the sea and rapidly slipped towards the bottom. Also arriving with them were simple molecules, most of which separated into ions on contact with the water.

They were all molecules made up of young atoms, born in a medium-size star like the Sun – only a bit older – which, when it died, had hurled part of itself into space before becoming a White Dwarf. This explained the large number of iron and carbon particles.

Cal went up to the newly arrived ions and immediately took to one of them, Potassium, a lad of two hundred and fifteen who was curious, inquisitive and impatient, like himself.

"Cal, I have to confess that we are an ignorant lot. Those particles of iron and carbon that you will have seen fall have been with us since birth. Very few of the old atoms, the hydrogens and the heliums, have travelled with us. We haven't had any teachers, so when we saw this giant asteroid appear... we were flabbergasted! Can you explain to me where we've ended up? No-one in the cloud could tell me."

Cal was about to give Potassium an explanation and thought of giving him a summary of the history of the Solar System and its planets, but straight away he realised that the task was impossible. Poor Potassium, who had recently turned into an ion, was still confused, and this was not the time to give him a lesson on the formation of planetary systems. So he said to him:

"There'll be time enough for explanations. I suggest that you take it easy and spend a bit of time exploring your new home. The water molecules will be your guide."

As he watched them go off, it occurred to Cal that maybe he could tell them one of his stories about human beings. He rather liked the idea. The time had come to pass on that unique experience to the younger atoms, something that he had suggested to himself when he was part of Francisco's shoulder-blade.

One week later Hydrogen was surrounded by some of the ions that had arrived in the stellar dust, amongst them Potassium. A bit further away, Cal, Selenium and the other atoms that accompanied them in their ions also attended the old sage's class. Hydrogen explained the secrets of the Universe, the formation of the stars, the particular case of the Sun and its planets, the laws of thermodynamics and of chemistry. Then he initiated them in the principles of electrochemistry, and many of them got very excited over the description of their behaviour as ions. Now they could understand what had happened to them when they dissolved in the sea water.

As he described the Solar System, Hydrogen explained that some planets, like the Earth, Mars, Saturn and Jupiter, had satellites that orbited around them. The easiest example to observe was the Moon, the Earth's only satellite. Then he went on to talk about the satellites of Mars, and when he got to

Saturn he amazed them with his description of the rings that used to go round it in times past. He said:

"It must be about eight hundred million years ago that they disappeared, slowly dispersing into space. It was a most unfortunate event because they were a unique sight in the Solar System."

When he mentioned that Saturn had over thirty satellites, Selenium asked Cal in a quiet voice so as not to interrupt:

"Do you remember the names of Saturn's satellites?"

"A few of them: Titan, the largest one; Rhea, Dione, but I can't remember the others."

"Don't you remember Phoebe?"

"Yes, now that you've reminded me. It's tiny, about two hundred kilometres in diameter and the one furthest away from the planet."

"I bet you don't know how Phoebe differs from the rest."

""No, I don't. Come on, Selenium, for pity's sake, I can't cope with all your facts."

"The fundamental difference is that all of the other satellites go round Saturn in the same direction and on a common plane, which is more or less the planet's equator. Phoebe, on the other hand, orbits in the opposite direction and on a different plane. What's more, the chemical composition of its surface is different from that of the others."

Cal hadn't taken in the importance of these differences, when Selenium added:

"The only explanation for this phenomenon is that Phoebe is not a satellite that was formed at the same time as the planet, as happened with all of the others, but was an errant comet that was wandering freely through space until it crossed paths with Saturn, was trapped by its gravitational field and couldn't escape."

When Selenium finished his explanation, Cal remained silent while he allowed his thoughts to focus on a fascinating, new idea.

At that moment Hydrogen, who was rather tired of talking, suggested to Cal that he tell one of his stories.

"That way they can amuse themselves a little and forget about the science for a while," he said.

The ions were very keen on the idea. Potassium was one of the most enthusiastic.

Cal proposed a short break, which gave him the chance to plan out his story. Then he began:

"I'm going to talk about human beings, which were very complex organisms made up of atoms like ourselves and which existed on this planet a very long time ago."

Hydrogen thought to himself: 'Cal managed it! He was able to form part of a human being! That atom is amazing!"

Before he started his story, which would go from scenes in the war to the gunshot that tore him out of Francisco's body, Cal felt that he ought to explain a certain basic facts about the human race. But no sooner had he started this introduction, when something unexpected happened: the same young atoms who, without any problem, had understood Hydrogen's ideas about physics, chemistry and thermodynamics couldn't take in the concept of *humans*. Cal's repeated attempts met with such little success that he didn't even manage to tell the story of the Spanish civil war. The idea of human beings turned out to be totally beyond them; the complexity of their organisms came across as absurd, redundant and unnecessary.

Cal made several further attempts to get them to understand, but they were all in vain. And when, as a last resort, he tried to explain the mechanism of reproduction on the basis of the sexes, the confusion was total. What's more, there were no longer any living creatures in the sea, so that Cal, who had to rely on memory, didn't have any examples to illustrate his explanations. Having failed, he made up some excuse and decided that the meeting was over.

If his first reaction was to doubt his abilities as a teacher, he quickly recalled how Oxygen had understood his ideas about creation and fate, as well as so many other occasions when other atoms had accepted his arguments. No, *he* wasn't the problem; there must be another reason. It then occurred to him that the difficulty that the young atoms had when they tried to understand the essence of human beings was on a par with the difficulty that human beings had when they tried to reveal the essential aspects of atoms. When they tried to discover the ultimate mystery, they failed to do so, and that's when they were overcome by uncertainty.

Cal felt the need to be alone. He was troubled by a dreadful thought: Had human beings really existed, or were they just the fruits of his imagination?

He came to his own defence: 'Human beings were on the Earth for a very short time. It was a brief, fleeting episode in the history of the planet. Since atoms don't dream, then I haven't been dreaming. They must have existed; Francisco and Roberto and all the others were real.' But a second later he contradicted himself: 'My thoughts could have invented them. In the nearly one billion years that I spent imprisoned in the concrete, time stopped for me. I assumed then that I could no longer think, but I probably did do so...'

He was tortured by anguish.

He decided to return to the surface of the sea to look at the sky. He allowed his atomic gaze to wander before holding it on a very bright star. He kept it held there for quite a while, until he found the idea he was looking for, the one that would be his solace. Then, as if to confirm his wish, he said in a very quiet voice:

"Within a few million years we'll reach that star, which will no doubt be young, like the Sun when I was a child. When we get close, the star will trap us and the earth will cease to be an enormous wandering rock and become a planet again. We'll start to dance around it and it will provide us with its warmth and its light. Dawns and dusks will return, together with the wind and the waves in the sea."

Selenium, who remained still at his side, listened until Cal finished his sentence.

"Do you seriously believe that that can happen to us?"

Cal's answer was restrained; he appeared to be talking to himself:

"Perhaps I just wish it with all my strength. Besides, have you forgotten the story of Phoebe that you yourself told me?"

"You're right; it is possible. If it were to happen, would you enter a human being again?"

"I don't think that the history of the Earth will repeat itself. If life were to develop again on the planet, there's no reason why it should be the same as the life that I knew. It would be an enormous coincidence to see it culminate in another human race."

"But suppose it does happen, from amino acids to human beings…"

"In that case, yes. But I wouldn't just be part of one. I'd get into his brain to give him advice. I'd warn him about the risks that the human race would run if they tried to repeat history. And I'd certainly tell him how intelligent beings were developed."

Selenium looked at the tiny dot that shone in the sky. It was like a promise.

"We'll only have to wait a few tens of millions of years," said Cal.

And they plunged down into the icy water.

GLOSSARY

ALPHA CENTAURI

The star system closest to the Sun, situated 4.5 light years away. It consists of three stars: Alpha Centauri A, which is yellow and slightly larger and older than the Sun; Alpha Centauri B, smaller and the same age. The two orbit around each other. The third star, Proxima Centauri (so called because it is the one closest to us) is a Red Dwarf that orbits around the two larger ones.

If Alpha Centauri A and the Sun were the size of an orange, they would be separated by a distance of about 2,000 kilometres.

ATOM

This is the basic element of all matter that exists in the Universe; water, air, vegetation, minerals, humans, are all made up of atoms. They are very small; if you could line them up side by side, you would need more than 10 million atoms to cover the distance of one centimetre.

An atom is a planetary system in miniature. It consists of a nucleus at its centre and electrons that revolve around it in concentric orbits and at different levels. In its turn the nucleus is made up of two distinct particles: the protons, which have a positive electrical charge, and the neutrons, which have no electrical charge. The electrons have a negative electrical charge. As a result atoms are electrically neutral because they have the same number of protons and electrons.

In fact the atomic structure is more complex, since the neutrons and the protons are in turn made up of a family of even more basic particles called quarks.

The atom is 10,000 times larger than its nucleus, and the nucleus (where almost all of the mass of the atom is concentrated) is 2,000 times larger than an electron. To put it another way, if an atom were the size of a football field, the nucleus would be the size of a ping-pong ball placed in the centre of the field and the electrons would be like grains of sand moving around in the stands. Virtually all matter is a large empty space.

Atoms differ from each other depending on the amount of protons that make up its nucleus. This amount is defined as its atomic number. A different chemical element corresponds to each number. In Nature there are 92 elements, although in the laboratory they have created a total of 106. The simplest element is hydrogen, whose nucleus is made up of 1 proton (without neutrons) and 1 electron. Hydrogen-2 or deuterium has 1 proton and 1 neutron in its nucleus and 1 electron; a helium atom has two protons and two neutrons in its nucleus and 2 electrons; a uranium atom has 92 protons and an equal number of electrons. Ninety-nine per cent of all visible matter in the Universe is made up of hydrogen and helium atoms; all of the other atomic elements constitute the remaining one per cent. The most abundant atoms are oxygen (whose nucleus has 8 neutrons and 8 protons, which are surrounded by 8 electrons) and the others are sodium, potassium, calcium, magnesium, carbon, iron, silicon, phosphorus, aluminium, chlorine, mercury, nickel, nitrogen, sulphur, gold and silver.

In the course of its evolution Nature has devised them in such a way that all known organic matter is made up of barely thirty atomic elements – an achievement equivalent to that of human beings who, with only twenty-six letters of the alphabet, have constructed hundreds of thousands of words, each one with a different meaning.

BINARY STARS

These are two companion stars, in other words, they are close to each other, reciprocally influenced by their respective fields and which revolve around a common centre of gravity. When they were formed the cloud of hydrogen gas that brought them into being was condensed into two centres instead of one as in the case of the Sun. It is estimated that between 30 and 40 per cent of the stars in the Universe belong to this category.

The image seen through existing telescopes shows only one star rather than two, since the distance means that the image merges them into a single star. The existence of binaries is deduced from spectrographic studies or eclipses that occur between the companion stars. When they are aligned in the observer's vision, the brightness diminishes, since one star casts a 'shadow' on the other.

Binary stars can also have planetary systems like the Solar System. For the hypothetical inhabitants of such planets sunrises and sunsets must look very unusual and very different from ours.

CALCIUM

One of the most widely known atomic elements. The calcium atom forms part of a large number of molecules that are the basis of very common substances in Nature, including calcium oxide, which is the lime used in construction; calcium carbonate or limestone; calcium sulphate or plaster; calcium phosphate, an important constituent of bones.

Its atomic nucleus is made up of 20 protons and 20 neutrons, around which revolve 20 electrons in orbits that form concentric layers.

CONSTELLATION

Each of the regions (groups of stars) into which human beings have divided the heavens in accordance with their observations from the Earth, attributing to each one a particular figure: the Dove, the Great Bear, the Three Marias, the Southern Cross…

The stars, nebulae and galaxies that make up the constellations have different degrees of brightness and different ages and are separated from the Sun by distances that vary from a few thousands to millions of light years. The only thing that these celestial bodies have in common is that they are located in the same field of vision for a terrestrial observer. If the observers of the sky were the inhabitants of another planet in the galaxy, their 'constellations' would be different. This idea can be made clear from the following example: a woman walks along a street and when she reaches a corner she looks up and sees a child standing opposite her; behind him, more than two hundred metres away she can see a tree in a nearby square. Her 'astronomic' conclusion will be: the child and the tree belong to the same constellation. A man walks along a street that forms a right-angle to the street that the woman was walking down, reaches the corner formed by both streets, looks up and sees the same child in profile;

behind the child he sees the dome of a church. His 'astronomic' conclusion will be: the child and the church belong to the same constellation.

Nowadays the constellations defined by ancient civilisations are useful for explaining where a particular body in the firmament is to be found. For example, the star Aldebaran lies in the constellation of Taurus.

Another very unusual division of the sky is the astrological one, which establishes twelve equal-angled sectors called signs of the Zodiac. Astrologers use this classification as a basis for their horoscopes. If an astrologer lived on another planet of the Milky Way, it would be difficult to imagine how, without contradicting himself, he would manage to assess the influences of the stars on the inhabitants of his planet.

GALAXY

A collection of stars, dust, gas and dark matter which is kept together by the force of gravity. There are several billion galaxies in the Universe. The number of stars that make up each galaxy varies between 10 million and 1 trillion.

Telescopes can enable galaxies to be detected that are 10 billion light years from the Earth. The average distance between two stars in the same galaxy is 4 to 5 light years; the distance between two neighbouring galaxies is about 2 million light years. For example, the distance between the Milky Way and the Andromeda galaxy (known as M31 to astronomers and which can be seen with the naked eye in the sky behind the constellation of the same name) is 2.9 million light years.

ION

The name given to every electrically charged atom or molecule. The explanation given here is confined to those ions that are found in saline solutions such as sea water.

All atoms of the different chemical species (except for the noble atoms, like Argon and the rest) tend to join together to form stable compounds called molecules. They can do so within species or with atoms from other species. So, two oxygen atoms join together to constitute an oxygen molecule which, together with nitrogen molecules, make up the air; two hydrogen atoms and one of oxygen combine to create a molecule of water; an atom of chlorine joins an atom of sodium to form a molecule of sodium chloride (common salt).

Atoms can combine in two ways, one of which is the electrovalent (or ionic) bond. For example, a chlorine atom has 7 electrons in its outer layer and sodium only has 1. In order for them to combine, sodium assigns its electron to chlorine, both are left with 8 electrons in their outer layer and acquire an electric charge (sodium a positive one, because it has a greater number of electrons than protons in its nucleus, and chlorine a negative one, for the opposite reason). These new particles created from the atoms are called ions. Positive ions are called cations and the negative ones, anions. In a solid state these ions remain joined together due to the electrical attraction between the two and constitute a sodium chloride molecule. A crystal of table salt is made up of millions of these molecules.

Although water molecules are electrically neutral, they have a polar character, that is, one end of the molecule is positive and the other negative. If sodium chloride is dissolved in water, the water molecules divide the sodium chloride molecules into its two ions and the ions become separate. The water molecules surround these ions as if protecting them at the same time as separating them. In order to do so they position their poles, the positive to the chloride ions and the negative to the sodium ones.

The molecules and the ions can be made up of more than two elements. For example the magnesium sulphate molecule consists of 1 atom of sulphur, 4 atoms of oxygen and 1 atom of magnesium. When dissolved in water it separates into two ions: a sulphate ion with 2 negative electric charges and a magnesium ion with 2 positive electric charges.

LIGHT YEAR

A unit of length used to measure distances in the Universe, corresponding to the distance that a light photon travels in a year. As light moves at a speed close to 300,000 kilometres per second, the distance of one light year is equivalent to 10 trillion (10 million million) kilometres. Here are some examples: the Milky Way is about 100,000 light years across; the star Sirius is 8 light years from the Earth.

The unit of longitude used by astronomers is the parsec, equivalent to 3.26 light years. For smaller distances, for example those within the Solar System, the Astronomic Unit (AU) is used. This is equal to the average distance between the Sun and the Earth (about 150 million kilometres) and equivalent to 8 light minutes. This means that the light given out by the Sun takes 8 minutes to reach the Earth. Examples: Jupiter is 5.2 AU from the Sun, while Pluto, the most distant planet in the Solar System, is 39.5 AU.

MOLECULE

The smallest particle into which a pure chemical substance can be divided while retaining its composition and properties (see ION).

A molecule is formed by the union of two or more atoms. This union can be electrovalent, as explained in relation to sodium chloride, or covalent. In the latter case the atoms that form it share the electrons of its outer layer, which always adds up to 8 in number. For example an atom of oxygen with 6 electrons in its outer layer is joined up with two hydrogen atoms, each with 1 electron in its outer layer, to create a molecule of water (the classic chemical formula of H_2O).

Some molecules are made up of a large number of atoms. For example the fluorescein molecule, which is a colorant, consists of twenty carbon atoms, twelve hydrogen atoms and five oxygen atoms.

One of the largest molecules to be found in nature is that of deoxyribonucleic acid (the familiar DNA of the genetic code) which is made up of thousands of atoms.

NEBULA OF ORION

Nebulae, which are very common in the Universe, are large concentrations of gases, mainly hydrogen and helium, and stellar dust. One of the best-known is the Nebula of Orion, which is very bright and beautiful and which can be seen in the middle of the constellation of the same name. Orion is 1,600 light years from the Earth and has a diameter of approximately 10 parsec. Its most interesting characteristic is that it is a region in space where very young stars can be seen surrounded by stellar dust, possibly in the first stage of the formation of its planetary systems.

PANGAEA (or Pangea)

In the Palaeozoic period, following a series of changes, the surface of our planet consisted of a large ocean Panthalassa, which covered three quarters of it, and a single mass of dry land, Pangaea, which occupied the remainder. After 40 million years without undergoing any change and towards the end of that geological period, Pangaea fractured along the line of the Equator, creating two continents: to the north Laurasia and to the south Gondwana. The ocean invaded the fracture and formed a narrow strait, the Tethys Ocean.

This process continued very slowly and produced other fractures. The most important was the one that separated the north-east of Brazil from the African territories of Nigeria and Cameroon. Eventually this long drawn-out break-up came to a halt and for 50 million years the Earth's surface has kept a shape which is similar to the present one. To understand the changes that the Earth's surface has undergone over time we need to explain that our planet, with a diameter of little more than 12,600 kilometres, does not have the physical characteristics of a solid and compact mass, but consists of a surface layer, the crust; another layer, the mantle, which supports the crust; and in the centre the nucleus. The thickness of the crust, which is rigid and very thin, is variable and may reach between 30 and 60 kilometres on the continents but less than 5 kilometres in certain parts of the ocean floor. The mantle is almost 3,000 kilometres thick and is a mass of semi-solid rock, with a density greater than that of the crust. The mantle has a very high temperature and the closer we get to the centre of the Earth the higher the temperature and the pressure. The nucleus is very dense as it is made of nickel and iron, and it is divided into two parts: the part that is beneath the mantle, which is liquid and is about 2,200 kilometres thick, and the nucleus itself, which is solid. The rotational action of the Earth causes the liquid nucleus to turn on the solid part and this relational movement is the origin of the Earth's magnetism. The crust is formed by rigid but independent tectonic plates that 'float' over the mantle. This causes the displacement of the continental masses. The relational movement of two plates against each other can create tensions in the boundary between them, causing possible earthquakes, volcanic eruptions and other telluric phenomena. These movements still occur and the plates continue to drift over the viscous mantle.

In our era the Atlantic Ocean is slowly getting wider at the same time that the Pacific is getting smaller in equal proportion, and some mathematical models forecast that within a few hundreds of millions of years a new Pangaea will be born again.

STAR

In the early stages of the formation of the Universe, practically all existing matter was made up of hydrogen and helium atoms. From its very beginnings the Universe has been expanding, in other words, it has been growing very fast in size – and according to measurements carried out in recent years, the speed of growth is increasing.

The expanding atomic clouds were not of a uniform density: in some regions of space the atoms were closer to each other. In these areas the hydrogen and helium atoms were forced by gravitational pull to get increasingly close to each other, and then the cloud turned into a dense mass of gas. The formation of a star in the Cosmos is due to this process of auto-compression which generates temperatures of several million degrees. When it reaches a certain critical condition, a nuclear reaction starts in the centre of the gaseous mass, which consists of the transformation of the atomic nuclei of hydrogen into nuclei of helium (in reality this process is much more complicated than what is described here). This reaction releases a massive amount of energy. The nuclear weapon known as a 'hydrogen bomb' is based on the same principle, with the difference that with the stars the process is self-regulating. The energy generated by the centre of the gaseous mass is cast into space in the form of radiation. Part of this radiation is the light emitted by the star - the closest example to us is the Sun. The energy that we receive from our star, and which enables life to exist on the Earth, is the product of a continuous and stable nuclear reaction.

Every star at birth has a certain quantity of hydrogen in its initial mass. With the passage of time the hydrogen gets used up as it turns into helium. At the end of the process the star slowly goes out until it dies. The end depends on the size of the star, in other words, on the quantity of hydrogen that made up its initial mass. If the size is the same or similar to that of the Sun, the star will slowly go out and will start to get bigger, turning itself into a red giant like those that today can be seen in their millions in the Universe. In this process of expansion it will absorb the planets that go round it, and therefore the existence of the Earth will come to an end. Then over millions of years the Sun will suffer successive contractions and expansions and an important part of its mass will be lost in space. Finally it will contract and it will turn into a white dwarf, a small dot in the sky. This whole process from the birth of the Sun until its death will take some 10 billion years. It is currently about half way through. If, on the other hand, the star is three or four times larger than the Sun, its life will be much shorter and its ending completely different.

Deprived of the strength that was provided by the nuclear reaction that developed in its nucleus, the star collapses due to the action of its own weight pulled by the force of gravity. Enormous pressures and temperatures are generated in its centre and the helium nuclei fuse with each other, resulting in the creation of the nuclei of heavier atoms like silicon, oxygen, carbon, calcium and all the rest. In the last act of its life, the star disintegrates in an extraordinary explosion and casts the whole of its mass into space in the form of cosmic dust. This is the incredible spectacle of a Supernova.

These giant stars have acted and continue to act as factories for the Cosmos, producing all of the atomic elements, except for hydrogen, helium and lithium (atoms that were formed at the beginning of the Universe and that help to create the stars, which in the last stage of their lives produce the other elements). The matter that today constitutes the Earth and its inhabitants was formed from these stars.

THE MILKY WAY

This is our galaxy, to which the Sun belongs - one of many in the vastness of the firmament. It is made up of 100 billion stars, some larger and some smaller than the Sun. Ancient peoples gave it its name because that it what it looked like: a milky white band, with a pale light, that covered the sky from one side to the other.

The Sun is close to the edge of its galaxy, about 30,000 light years from its centre, where it is believed that there is a black hole, a devourer of stars, which has entrapped the stars closest to it and will continue to do so in the future.

The Milky Way forms part of a group of about 30 neighbouring galaxies, called the Local Group by astronomers. Amongst them the Andromeda Galaxy stands out because of its size; it is spiral in shape and consists of double the number of stars in the Milky Way. The remaining galaxies are much smaller in size, or dwarf galaxies, such as Sagittarius, Ursa Minor, the Triangulum and the Magellanic Cloud amongst others.

The so-called Local Group lies at the edge of a large conglomeration that covers almost 5,000 galaxies. This cluster, which is huge given its size and the number of stars that it consists of, including the Sun and the Planet Earth, is nevertheless insignificant compared to the enormity of the

Cosmos, since its total mass represents barely a millionth part of the known universe.

UNIVERSE (Cosmos)

The Universe is a space-time continuum in which life evolves, with all of the matter and energy of which it is composed. Carl Sagan defined the surface of the earth as its boundary with the Cosmos.

The magnitude of the Universe and the corresponding smallness of our planet can be appreciated when looking at the heavens. The ability of human beings to study the sky has developed in an extraordinary way in recent decades thanks to the powerful range of the new telescopes available to astronomers (amongst the most outstanding is the Hubble Space Telescope). The difference between the new telescopes and the old ones is the same as the difference between opera glasses and a telescope used by a sailor.

It is important to make clear here that the images of the objects that are observed in the sky are of different ages, since the images have to travel through space at a finite speed before reaching the Earth. Therefore they are not current images, but rather representations of what these celestial bodies were like in the past. The further the observed body is from the Earth, the older the image. For example, we see the

Sun as it was 8 minutes ago, which is the time its light takes to reach the Earth; we see Jupiter as it was 43 minutes ago, Sirius as it was 8 years ago and the Nebula of Orion as it was 1,600 years ago. The image of the furthest galaxy that we know of is 10 billion years old. Looking at the sky at night is like travelling towards the past in a time-machine, because it enables us to cover the history of the Universe from its birth to the present day. We can see how one star was born and how another died; how the planetary systems were formed, how a Supernova exploded. People are seeing what the most distant star was like millions of years ago and what the nearest star was like 4 and a half years ago (as in the case of Alpha Centauri). These are the times that it takes for the images to reach the human eye after travelling through space at the speed of light (300,000 kilometres per second or 1,080 million kilometres per hour).

It has been calculated that the origin of our universe occurred in an initial act about 13,700 million years ago. At the time of the publication of this book science has not yet managed to explain what happened in the first milliseconds of its existence.

Works Consulted

Adams, Fred and Laughlin, Gregory. Sessions of the *American Association for* *the Advancement of Science*, 17 to 22 February 2000 (University of Michigan).

Asimov, Isaac. *Atom*, New York, Penguin Books, 1992.

Asimov, Isaac. *The Universe, from Flat Earth to Quasars,* New York, Walker, 1966.

Asimov, Isaac. *The Beginning and the End* , New York, Doubleday, 1977.

Biondi, Herman et al. *Rival Theories of Cosmology*; Oxford University Press, 1960.

Biondi, Herman. *The Universe at Large,* New York, Doubleday and Company Inc, 1960.

Crick, Francis. *The Astonishing Hypothesis (The Scientific Search for the Soul)*, New York, Simon & Schuster, 1994.

Dawkins Richard, *The God Delusion,* Boston, New York, Houghton Mifflin Company, 2006.

Drexler, Eric. *Engines of Creation*, New York, Doubleday, 1986.

Duquesne, Maurice. *Matter and Antimatter* , London, Arrow, 1960.

Feynman, Richard. *Six Easy Pieces*, Boston, Perseus Books, 1994.

Feynman, Richard. *The Character of Physical Law*, New York, Modern Library   Edition, 1994.

Gangui, Alejandro. *El Big Bang, la génesis de nuestra cosmología actual*, Buenos Aires, Eudeba, 2005.

Garlik, Mark. *The Story of the Solar System*, Cambridge, University Press, 2002.

Gribbin, John. *The Search for Superstrings, Symmetry and the Theory of   Everything*, Boston, Little Brown and Co., 1999.

Grinspoon, David. *Lonely Planets*, New York, Harper Collins Publishers, 2003.

Hawking, Stephen. *A Brief History of Time from the Big Bang to Black Holes*,   New York, Bantam Books, 1988.

Horgan, John. *The End of Science*, New York, Broadway Books, 1997.

Hubble telescope images. *http://hubblesite.org*

Jastrow, Robert. *Until the Sun Dies*, New York, W.W.Norton and Company,   1977.

Jastrow, Robert. *Stars, Planets and Life*, London, Heinemann, 1968.

Kaku, Michio y Trainer, Jennifer. *Beyond Einstein*, New York, Bantam Books,   1987.

Kaku, Michio. *Parallel Worlds*, New York, Double Day, 2005.

Krauss, Lawrence. *Atom*, Boston, Little, Brown & Co, 2001.

Kurzweil, Ray. *The Age of Spiritual Machines*, New York, Penguin Putman   Inc., 1999.

Kurzweil, Ray. *The Singularity is Near*, New York, Viking Penguin, 2005.

Lewis, John. *Worlds without End*, Boston, Perseus Books, 1998.

Mulhall, Douglas. *Our Molecular Future*, New York, Prometheus Books, 2002.

Rees, Martin. *Just Six Numbers*, New York, Basic Books, 2000.

Rees, Martin. *Our Final Hour*, New York, Basic Books, 2003.

Reeves, Hubert. *Poussières d'étoiles*, Paris, Editions du Seuil, 1994.

Reston, James. *Orion, where Stars are Born*, National Geographic Magazine,   Volume 186, 6, 1995.

Sagan, Carl. *Cosmos*, London, Mac Donald, 1980.

Susskind Leonard. *The Cosmic Landscape*, New York, Little Brown and   Company, 2006.

The Planetary Society, http://*planetary.org/home*

Vilar, Pierre. *La guerra civil española*, Barcelona, Grijalbo Mondadori, 1986.

Ward, Peter and Brownlee, Donald. *The Life and Death of Planet Earth, New*   York, Henry Holt, 2004.

CONTENTS

INTRODUCTION

www.ingramcontent.com/pod-product-compliance
Lightning Source LLC
Chambersburg PA
CBHW052026020726

47501CB00004B/1270